SLADE'S GLACIER

SLADE'S

GLACIER

BY ROBERT F. JONES

Skyhorse Publishing

Skyhorse Publishing books may be purchased in bulk at special discounts for sales promotion, corporate gifts, fund-raising, or educational purposes. Special editions can also be created to specifications. For details, contact the Special Sales Department, Skyhorse Publishing, 307 West 36th Street, 11th Floor, New York, NY 10018 or info@skyhorsepublishing.com.

Skyhorse® and Skyhorse Publishing® are registered trademarks of Skyhorse Publishing, Inc.®, a Delaware corporation.

Visit our website at www.skyhorsepublishing.com.

10 9 8 7 6 5 4 3 2 1

Library of Congress Cataloging-in-Publication Data is available on file.

ISBN: 978-1-62873-783-7
Ebook ISBN: 978-1-62914-155-8

Cover design by Brian Peterson

Printed in the United States of America

FOR CHARLES F. JONES
(1905–1980)
"Up North"

PROLOGUE

That country is best approached from the sea, the ship ghosting shoreward through a fogbank, her deck and hull beaded, fresh water dripping from sheets and halyards. Then the gray light breaking toward blue: tatters of fog braid the rigging. Somewhere to starboard sea lions bark—hollow yaps and honks, as if the fog were mourning its own demise. Now the light brightens rapidly and the sun shows like a worn coin through the thinning mist. Finally, to break clear and see the country rising dead ahead, its raw and awful power.

Not just the size, but the enormity of it: a country that can rape at a glance. That black-green, bristling coast—hemlock, cedar, Sitka spruce—hunkered under the vast glare of mountains, slashed with falling water, punctuated in ice. An offshore wind butts the fogbank seaward; whales blow rainbows against the light. A square mile of ocean erupts, frolics, disappears: porpoises at play. Closer inshore, sea otters dive through swaying yellow forests of kelp, then float on their backs, grinning, as they crack spider crabs and toss aside the sucked husks.

Sudden bait balls—a million herring compressed by panic, ten-foot globules of instinctive fear, circling and circled, hit and ripped by the sea lions so that the tilting black surface of the sea is spangled in scales. A scraw of seabirds overhead— fulmar and shearwater, gull and tern, jaeger and skua—and now a gam of Orcas, killers in black-and-white dinner dress, coursing in from the fogbank to slam the sea lion herd: tendrils of blood thinning toward yellow. The tall dorsals slash and gleam and zigzag. Hit by a killer whale, a great bull spins skyward, silent, his dog's eyes going dim as he falls to the waiting maw.

Alaska.

Take this for the truth: Any man who says he is not frightened by his first glimpse of it is either a fool or a liar.

A slow swell rolls shoreward, turning from green and black to murky brown as it surges up the tidal flat, breaking at last on the lustrous mud and leaving behind its loops and coils of foam: sea snakes built of tan bubbles that shiver to the thud of succeeding waves. Above the high-tide mark, the beach is shingle and sea wrack: smooth, skull-sized boulders thatched with scarred logs—escapees from coastal lumber rafts—and tangles of driftwood, all meshed and snarled with tentacles of rotting kelp.

This coast is rich in life and death. A billion generations of mollusks and arthropods died to build the beach: razor clams and butter clams, king crabs and Dungeness crabs, whelks and snails and abalone and goose barnacles. Beyond the reach of the surf, the ribs of a fin whale, bleached by salt and time to polar whiteness, arch like an untented canopy over a single vertebra, broad as a tea table. There are human bones as well, buried now by the undertaking sea. Haida and Tlingit and Aleut bones; the bones of once-bearded Russians, traders in fur for Aleksandr Baranov's Russian-America Company, massacred upriver by the Tlingit, their skulls split and guts jellied by fiercer blows than those of their own knouts and *nagaikas*, those favored instruments of Tsarist commerce. The *promyshleniki* of the Russian-America Company justified their excesses with an old proverb: "God is on high and the Tsar is far away." But the Tlingit, unlike the timid Aleuts whom the Russians had enslaved on their way east, were near and fearless.

Closer to the surface lie the bones of American gold seekers and the rusting absurdity of their machines: buried in sea tangle, nearly invisible now, a great red steam car flakes away in silence. It had been meant to carry men and gear across the mountains to the mother lode; it never cleared the beach.

Behind the rusting behemoth rises a wall of coastal forest, rooted in ten thousand years of dead and decaying conifers. Trees grow from trees, tiny saplings sprout from the moss that devours their ancestors. Walking the forest floor is impossible unless one follows the pleached and sinuous thoroughfares of the brown bears—one of whom might be ambling bemusedly around the next bend. The only safe way through this tangle of spikes and bears is to follow up the fiord of the Alugiak River as it drains to the sea from ice-capped mountains now invisible through the timber.

The fiord itself is quiet, windless, its surface broken only occasionally by the roll of a salmon. Hair seals bark and argue on the rocks that line the shore. The Alugiak itself, brawling and bouldered, decants from the forest with a white-water roar. From below, the rapids look impassable: great transverse ribs of granite studded with boulders the size of houses; gushers of beer-brown water crashing and caroming down the chutes; dead trees piled athwart a gap, one spruce snag standing upright, skinned, throbbing and humming to the water's blows. But salmon climb these falls and so can men. By lining and poling a canoe up the right hand side of the rapids, it is possible to reach the top with only one carry.

From the head of the rapids, the country opens out into a wide, gently climbing valley that angles inland to the northeast. The protective girdle of blowdowns and devil's club gives way to parklike grassland studded with islands of spruce, birch and aspen. Along the brush-bearded course of the river grow giant ferns and willow. Pale huckleberries and cloudberries, red and yellow salmonberries, wild apple and dogwoods a hundred feet tall find footing along the edges of valley. Farther upstream, the country grows wetter: a maze of sloughs and pothole ponds, creeks and mucky rivulets, muskeg and true tundra. At every step of elevation lie kettle moraines and mounds of ice-scoured gravel.

At the far end of the valley, tucked in a crotch of the distant mountains, waits the engineer of this landscape: a cubic mile of blue-green ice. As Alaskan glaciers go, this one is nothing remarkable. It lacks the sprawl and spectacle of the Mendenhall or the Malaspina farther south. You cannot run a steamboat up to its snout, as you can at Glacier Bay, and with a blast on the ship's whistle send great icebergs calving into the sea. Yet in its day, a hundred centuries ago, this glacier was the dominant force and feature of the country. It filled the valley: a great, broad-shouldered, rumble-gutted river of blue ice more than thirty miles long and five wide, its undulating back, half a mile above bedrock, covered with rock and dirt and stands of living trees, its nose in the sea, its ragged fangs flaking off to generate waves that could swamp a war canoe.

The Tlingit payed homage whenever they passed, wishing it good health and asking it for favors. Like early Europeans, who saw glaciers as ice dragons, the Tlingit knew the ice to be animate—a giant blue bear that moved slowly but with irresistible power. The Tlingit believed that the universe was made up of a few orderly sequences of cause and effect— shoot enough arrows and the moose dies—plus an enormous amount of something unpredictable that they called *yek*. *Yek* was the head of a shark, decapitated hours ago, suddenly snapping off the foot of a man who playfully kicked at it. *Yek* was the whim of the Thunderbird, causing lightning to flash from his eyes on a clear day. The earth was a plate of water, rock and ice, balanced on a long pole by The Old Woman Underneath. The Old Woman was nervous, and when she twitched, the earth shook, the mountains fell and the sea arose to suck down whole villages. That too was *yek*.

As the glacier slowly retreated up the valley from the sea, vast lakes of ice melt accumulated behind its ever thinning walls. When they broke, the water crashed down the valley, tumbling trees and rocks and Tlingit and their community houses along with it. The drowned and shattered bodies of moose and bear and Dall sheep rolled with the flood. Now and then the distorted, bug-eyed faces of uprooted totem poles rose from the whirling scum, stared briefly, then surged head-first below. That was powerful *yek*, indeed. The Tlingit left the river.

Now, in its old age, the glacier was relatively benign. It squatted at the head of the valley, its shoulders wedged between two mountain slopes. Its mile-wide front beetled high over a terminal moraine of boulders, talus, scree and gray glacial mud. A dozen small streams gushed from under its skirt, milky water freighted with grit, and combined to form the Alugiak River. The wall of the glacier was sculpted by weather into a crenellated surface where mutant armies clash on melting legs, their warped swords and hammers frozen in midswing. Misshapen gods weep blue tears that redden at sunset. Smooth-walled caves lead into the ice, turning and twisting as if bored by some giant worm, only to end against blank walls that glow blue and green in the light filtering from above. Now and then frozen carcasses emerge slowly from the glacier's maw: the bodies of animals fallen into crevasses long ago, before the days of men.

Other secrets lie hidden beneath the ice, awaiting their moment of revelation in the long thaw. Sometimes the milky water that leaks from beneath the glacier wears a rainbow sheen, and the riverbanks downstream glow iridescent in the low last light. There is oil down there. This, of course, is not unusual in Alaska, difficult as it may be to realize that once, on these sun-lorn lands of rock and ice and stunted trees, great leafy forests grew in the ancient greenhouse of the planet. How much oil, though, is the big question.

You might stand there, oily muck on your boots, and stare at the ice wall. The real strike—the great pool—is back there: back up the groin of the mountain, buried under a million million tons of ice. You would slap distractedly at a moose fly circling your head, wipe the sweat from your brow (it is hot at the glacier's front in midsummer: the ice is a warped mirror). You would stare again, up the ice wall to the over-hanging lip high above, dripping and translucent against the hot sky. After a while you might laugh. A fine joke, this one. A fortune lying in there, irretrievable: like those medieval tales of dragons sleeping on pots of gold. Tickle this dragon, and he would respond with a thousand tons of crashing ice.

That night there is a full moon and the glacier rears above the camp, a baleful presence shot through with pale light, the frontal seracs gleaming like fangs in the moonlight. In the silence you can hear the streams of melt gurgling out from under the ice. You rise from the fire and work the bolt of your rifle, sliding a round into the chamber. Just as an experiment, you squeeze the trigger, aiming randomly skyward, watching the glacier.

The shot roars down the valley.

The glacier groans, then screams.

A tower of ice teeters in the moonlight, then falls with a splintering roar to the rocks and mud below. . . .

The Tlingit would have loved it.

PART ONE

JACK SLADE

1950

CHAPTER ONE

"**G**ET A load of this," said Healey.

The window looked out on the tarmac where the planes were parked. A man in a full-length bearhide coat walked toward the office dragging something on a leash. It was a squat, wide, thickly furred animal, its jaws lashed tight over a stick secured with rawhide thongs.

At every other step the animal turned and lunged at the man. The man stopped, cursed mechanically, and kicked the animal in the chops.

The animal could have been a small bear but it had a flat head and too long a tail and yellowish stripes ran from its forehead down along the sides of its glossy dark brown pelt. Its eyes were pure flashing fire.

The man came into the office.

"How much you charge to take this critter to Fairbanks?" He was bearded and weathered and smelled like a salmon cannery. The animal growled and lunged.

The man kicked it.

"What the hell is it?" Healey asked.

"Carcajou," the man said. "Injun Devil. What you'd call a wolverine. I promised Doc Haggs up in Fairbanks that I'd get one for him. Took me all winter to outsmart this son of a bitch and most of the spring to walk him into town."

"Sixty cents a pound for freight," said Healey. "How much does he weigh?"

"Be damn if I ever put him on a scale," the trapper said. "Probably about forty, fifty pound. You want to weigh him, go ahead."

"I'll take your word for it. Charge you forty bucks plus another five to crate him. Make it fifty since we'll have to keep an eye on him in case he gets airsick."

"Ain't got no fifty," the trapper said. "And he won't get sick 'cause he ain't et since last Tuesday when he got holt of my winter mukluks. But I'll give you eight beaver. Full blanket beaver."

"Ten," Healey said.

"Eight," said the trapper, "and I'll crate him for you."

"We're flying up that way this afternoon," Healey told him. "There's lumber and tools in that quonset over by the plane."

For the next hour we could hear the man hammering and cursing while the wolverine growled and scrabbled. Then the man came back into the office and flopped a stack of peltry on the table. "That ought to hold him," he said. "I took a couple extra turns of babiche over his muzzle. You don't want him getting loose."

"We've hauled pigs and bears," Healey said. "Once we took a crate of eagles down to Ketchikan."

"A bear's a sissy compared to a carcajou," the trapper said. "You keep an eye on him he don't get loose. He'll eat up your plane and use the wings for toothpicks."

"What's your name?" I asked him. "I'll need it for the bill of lading."

"The Mad Trapper," he said. "Tell Doc Haggs the Mad Trapper. He'll know who I am. Give him a copy of the freight bill and tell him to send the money order to the Blue Bear down in town. I'm going to hang out there for a while, get good and shitfaced, fuck me some of them dollies from the cannery. The Mad Trapper."

There were three or four Mad Trappers in that country back

then. They all took the name from the original Mad Trapper, a hard case named Albert Johnson who killed a Mountie over the line in the Yukon back in the early thirties and was himself killed on a frozen oxbow of the Eagle River after a long midwinter chase through the Richardsons. The Mounties had to shoot him seven times before he would die, and even at that he wounded three of them. I saw a photograph of him once that they'd taken after they killed him. A snub-nosed, jug-eared little guy, his dead eyes slitted and glaring, pale, his pale hair frozen in wild cowlicks, a scruffy beard bristling around his final, baretoothed grimace: like an animal clubbed to death in a trap. Like a blond carcajou.

CHAPTER TWO

HEALEY AND I came into that country right after the war. We'd flown together in the China–Burma–India theater with the Air Transport Command and the only alternative when the war ended was flying for the airlines. Neither of us could have stuck it. Too much like driving a cab. So we pooled our savings—mainly Healey's—and bought a war-surplus C-47 Dakota and headed up into Alaska to take a crack at the bush pilot business. We'd settled down pretty steady in Gurry Bay, a cannery town on the Gulf of Alaska where the Dead Mountie Range peels off inland from the Chugach. Business was good in those years right after the war and we carried everything from whores to gold dredges all over the place. The government built a slew of airfields and weather stations during the war and you could land almost anywhere. It was good flying, you had to stay on your toes, though, with that weather changing the way it did, but the country was tough and gorgeous and we got in a lot of hunting and fishing. The women weren't much and most of the locals were tough old bones with livers the size of their boots, but we liked it up there and we thought we knew what we were doing.

We took off that afternoon when the fog lifted but got right back into it at a hundred feet. Then it broke clear and we could see the country all around. Ice and black rock and cold steel water, big sprawling stretches of black-needled spruce, one little salmon seiner pounding north like a chip of pine up through the channel toward Cordova. Mighty empty. We'd flown the Hump for three years and that was empty country too.

Healey was a big lop-eared, easygoing guy who kidded around a lot and played a canny game of poker. Women had told him he looked like Clark Gable and he grew a little blond cookie-duster to enhance the likeness. He loved India, the bright hot stench of it, the fiery food, the swarthy squirming monkey-bodied girls with rhinestones in their noses, and the big slow dusty cattle wandering vacant-eyed through the crowded bazaars, and off in the distance the faint wink of ice high in the Himalayas.

On the other side of the mountains was China. K'un-ming was cold, crowded and poorer even than India. In the morning in front of the hotel where the pilots stayed you would see beggars frozen in the gutter. I kicked one once and he crackled. Sometimes you would see camel caravans in from central Asia, tall knock-kneed mangy animals hung with tiny brass bells and ridden by wiry little men carrying blackpowder rifles. If you knew the right people, you could make a lot of money in K'un-ming. Healey knew them. He sold them nylons, cigarettes, British booze and sometimes opium and by the time the war ended he had fifty grand in his kick. Before the war, he'd knocked around the Middle West selling insurance and tending bar. Now he was rich and he knew how to fly.

The war had been good to me, too, but in another way. It took me off the dirt-poor mountain farm in Vermont where I'd have been busting my balls to this day, and it fed me better than I'd ever eaten before, and it pinned gold bars on my collar and wings on my chest. But mainly it showed me the way into empty country.

Ever since childhood I have been in love with empty places. I had no playmates, not even a brother or sister, only my books, my rifle and the mountains. When my chores were done,

I wandered the ridges above the farm in all weather, hunting out forgotten caves and abandoned cellar holes, excavating ancient dumps and salvaging old tools: broad-ax heads, adzes, crosscut saw blades, rusty milk jugs, handblown brown and green bottles, once a fine long octagon barrel from a squirrel rifle. These, I painstakingly restored and hoarded in my loft bedroom, until one day my mother sold them to an antique dealer (keeping the money for herself).

Mainly, though, I loved the solitude, the taking care of myself in hard country. I fished the brooks with a burlap sack, spreading the mouth with rocks and twigs at the outlet of a trout pool and then spooking the "natives" (as we called brook trout) into it by disturbing the pool itself. Three or four pools produced enough squirming, gleaming six-inchers for a meal, which I fried over an open fire in a pan I'd found high on the mountain. I learned where the squirrels and rabbits used, and the deer, and took them at any season with rifle or snare. Often, in good weather, I climbed to the top of the three-thousand-foot mountain and lay on the bare, lichen-grown rock reading a book of adventure from the town library: Baker's hunting stories from Ceylon, Selous on southern Africa, Sheldon pursuing the Arctic sheep, the journals of Lewis and Clark. Kipling, who once lived in Vermont, was well represented in the library, and I can still recite whole passages of *Kim* from memory. Jack London, though, was my favorite and I yearned with all a boy's aching ardor to see that harsh cold country "North of Fifty-three." To be coursing the crisp snow behind my own dogs with the Aurora blazing overhead and the wolves howling all around us as we ran—that would be heaven.

Though my father was a man of few words and fewer emotions, I believe he shared my dream. Often he would tell me about the Vermont of his youth, when there were still wolves and panthers and many more bears than we ever saw sign of. But the farm had him, and he the farm, and his time was taken with work and sleep. But he was of a strongly independent bend of mind, that hard old man. On the far end of our land there was a flat rock that had a gigantic footprint in it. One summer a group of scientists came and said it was a dinosaur's footprint. The state chose to exercise the right of eminent domain and take the farm for a park. They told my father he would have to accept the price they set.

That night, he went out and planted dynamite under the rock. I helped him drill the holes and place the charges. When the state delegation showed up the next morning in their fancy buggies and suits and ties, he blew it up.

Ker-pow! A sky full of dinosaur toenails.

Get fucked, he told them.

CHAPTER THREE

*W*E WERE clear of the spruce flats along the coast and well past the big rapids where the Alugiak River pours out of the Dead Mounties when the wolverine got loose. We had him caged back there with a couple of new Gray Marine diesel engines and two drums of av-gas and a few dozen cases of canned goods we were hauling to Fairbanks. The first thing we knew, the plane began to shake as if we'd been caught in clear air turbulence. Then we heard a kind of grating, ripping sound and we worried that an engine was tearing loose from its mount. But the wings held steady and the rivets looked sound so it wasn't that. Then we heard him growl. You couldn't mistake it. A kind of low, vibrant metallic grumble like a stick of bombs makes when they hit a target thousands of feet below you and you feel the explosions rapping on the belly of the plane, but then escalating into a higher, deeper ripping sound, as of saws through punky hardwood.

"Oh no," moaned Healey. "It's that frigging fur ball."

The fuselage jolted and shuddered.

"We'd better shoot him," I said.

"You shoot him," Healey said. "I'm not going back there."

I took the .45 and jacked a round into the chamber and opened the hatch. It was dark in there and the wolverine went quiet. I closed the hatch.

"Can't see him. And if I shoot, I might hit that fuel."

"Take a flashlight."

I shone the beam back into the hold and I saw his eyeshine, hard yellow, and then he ducked behind one of the engine crates.

"I'll have to go back in there."

"You're a better man than I am, pally."

I crawled back into the hold. The wolverine had smashed the canned goods all over the cargo deck. My knees squished around in creamed corn and green peas. There was a stink of Spam all through the hold. I poked the flashlight beam into all the corners but I couldn't see him.

Then I saw him.

He was coming for me, fast, with a low growl and his teeth glinting in the light beam. I got out as quick as I could, but not before he'd ripped my hand and grabbed the flashlight. We could hear him eating it—crunch, crunch, tinkle.

"Why didn't you shoot him?"

"Sure. Where's the first aid kit?"

"Back in the hold!" Healey was laughing.

I ripped off the sleeve of my shirt and wrapped it tight around the holes on the back of my hand. The blood was coming fast and now the pain was setting in. They have a strong jaw, those wolverines. We could hear him banging on the hatch right behind us. Up until I'd opened it that first time, he didn't know we were there. Now he knew and he wanted us. We could hear him digging and ripping up aluminum back there.

"Oh shit oh dear," Healey said. He wasn't laughing now. "Look at the oil pressure." It was flattening out to zero. "He got the feed line or something. Doesn't it run through back there?"

"You'd better pick a place to put her down," I told him. The engines would seize up in a couple of minutes. Healey wheeled around in a big circle to the right, banking her over so we could scout the ground. It was all mountain peaks and glaciers down there. None of them looked very flat. The starboard engine chugged and farted blue smoke, then quit. We were falling fast now and I saw a glacier coming up that looked fairly level. Big black unitaks stuck up through it like granite tree stumps but near the edge where it joined the face of the mountain it was pretty well free of obstacles. A long black moraine ran like a racing stripe just in from the rock.

"Put her down near the moraine," I said. "Bobby Reeve told me there's not so many crevasses near the edge. And if they're there, they're shallower and narrower than the ones in the middle of the glacier." Reeve was the guy who invented glacier landings. We'd never tried one before, but now there was no choice.

"Goddammit," Healey said, laughing again. "Shot down by a frigging what-you-may-call-it? What did that guy say it was called? A kinkajou?"

"Carcajou. Indian Devil."

"Shot down by a frigging carcajou. Who'd of thunk it?"

The port engine froze.

It was dead quiet except for the whistle of air over the fuselage and the ripping creaking sounds from the cargo deck where the wolverine was eating the plane. The ice came up to meet us like falling off a roller coaster, sun breaking like daggers on the blue ice, the surface of the glacier coming clear now, covered with small boulders and big streaks of dirt, some of them with spruce trees growing out of them, the ice wrinkled and bent and shot with big holes, then nose up and tail heavy with the wheel in his gut to scrub off airspeed, Healey touched her down, thump-clank-screech, and we were skidding sideways, around again, gear up and the props bent backward, one engine wiggling like a loose tooth in the socket of the wing, thump again, and we were stopped.

"Switches off?"

"On the way down," he said. "When the other engine went."

"That was sweet."

"I love you too."

CHAPTER FOUR

THE QUESTION now was how to get out of the plane. We couldn't take our leave by the side door, our usual mode of exit, because the wolverine was still back there. Fortunately the tool kit was in the cockpit and Healey unscrewed the window panels, skinning his knuckles and cursing all the while (he never was much good with tools), and we were able to hang by our hands and drop down into the snow that covered the glacier. It was cold and clear. All we had on was our long johns, khakis, coveralls and the old air corps leather flight jackets that were sheepskin-lined, but didn't cover your ass. No hats. No boots. Just sneakers.

"We've got to get that bastard out of there," Healey said.

"Can't open the cargo door from the outside."

The radio had broken on the crash landing and we hadn't been able to get off a May Day, so it didn't look like help was going to come winging in anytime soon.

"We'll have to rip a hole in the fuselage and hope he comes out."

"We'll be a couple of popsicles if he doesn't," Healey said. "Jack-O, my boy, we're in trouble."

There was a dead spruce snag over near the cliff, and I broke chunks off of it and started a fire in the lee of a big lichen-blotched boulder. That way, at least, we could avoid popsicle paradise. The plane had been intended for the Russian front and was painted white. Apart from stenciling the fuselage with our corporate name—Conundrum Airways—and a logo of a grizzly bear scratching its head, we had not repainted it. Perfect camouflage. Even if aircraft flew by every hour, it was unlikely that anyone would see us. All we had were the clothes we stood in, the .45 caliber Colt Model 1911-A automatic pistol I'd stolen from the air corps and with which I'd failed to assassinate the wolverine, two packs of Kools and Healey's Zippo lighter. There was a load of food in the plane, along with tarps and boots and sleeping bags and a bottle of Courvoisier brandy and a .30-caliber Johnson rifle that I'd bought in Delhi from an old Marine Corps warrant gunner toward the end of the war—swapped him, actually, for a case of Ballantine Scotch in the days when Ballantine was still worth drinking, before they thinned it and lightened it and took the hair off its balls.

But the wolverine was in there.

"I've got to plug that son of a bitch," I said.

"Be careful," Healey said. "I'll tend the fire. And don't shoot up the plane too bad. We're underinsured."

Samuel Patrick Healey was a dreadful man in many ways, as he proved to me later, but there was no way to hate him. He didn't care what he said, and when he said it, you had to laugh. In a land like Alaska, where everyone is honest, he was the truest of them all, even though he was a cheat and a coward and a backstabbing double dealer from the word go. I loved him then and I love him now, when I'm going to kill him.

But that was long, long ago. We dragged a treetrunk over to the cockpit and I climbed back into her. There was silence in the hold. I found the flashlight, badly gnawed, but working. The batteries were starting to fade but it was better than nothing, and I crawled in, the .45 slippery in my clenched palm.

Over the years, I have gone in after bigger animals, animals that could rip you from asshole to armpit with one lightning slash, a wounded brown bear once in a tangle of devil's club on the coast across from Afognak where you had to get down on your belly and inch your way into the green gloom, cold water dripping down your neck, the dank reek of skunk cabbage and drying bear blood in your nose, poking a .375 ahead of you and hoping he was dead, and if he wasn't, that you could shoot straight in that one damp tangled brown hairball of an instant when he came, but never—not even the day I dangled from my fingernails in a thousand feet of empty air and the Dall ram stamped at my hands over there in the Mounties— did I feel the hair stand as stiff as it did that late afternoon on the glacier when I went in for the carcajou.

I couldn't see him but I sure could smell him. He'd crapped on everything in the hold. The smell was mixed in with the smell of peas and beets and corn and baked beans, and it had that same reek of bones and old hair and the guts of a moose coming up through the skiffs of snow in August that you smell when you go into an old wintering yard in the country back of Platinum Bay, where there aren't any wolves left. I could feel him all around me. Silence. I crawled clear back to one of the diesel engine crates and climbed up onto it. The wind was working on the plane and for a while all I could hear was the squeak of flexing aluminum and the bumping of blood in my temples. Then I heard a kind of hissing, purring sound from the darkness behind me.

I turned around very carefully with my thumb on the hammer of the pistol and stared back into the black. Gradually, he emerged from it, a denser kind of blackness, solid, like when you have a fever and you can feel your teeth getting thicker and thicker in your throat, tasting like oiled mahogany, bitter, and I shut off the failing flashlight. Yes, I could see him better in the dark than in the light. I could make out the flat snaky wide head and his shoulders bunched in heavy dense coils and hear the rasp of his breath. The sight picture through the shallow notch of the .45's barrel was clear enough. I was square on the inch of space between his eyes.

They had a flat, barely visible sheen to them, not a glint

so much as a shimmer, unblinking, steady, the essence of wild malevolence. I felt myself starting to shake. Just as the hammer snapped, the eyes moved.

The roar of the .45 slammed my ears and filled the hull of the Dakota with an instant of nova. I blinked. Of course I'd missed him.

"Get him yet?"

It was Healey, leaning in the cockpit window with his Clark Gable kisser about to break into a laugh.

"No."

"Listen, you dim shit. I'm cold out here. Go get that damned weasel and kill it and then throw me my sleeping bag. As long as you're about it, throw down that brandy bottle too. What do you think I'm paying you for?" He growled with mock rage and went back down the treetrunk.

I stood there shaking and feeling hollow. Then I went over and threw the dogs on the cargo hatch and swung the door open. Light and fresh air poured into the plane and right away I felt better. While I was collecting unruptured cans of food and our emergency packs the wolverine kept still. I could hear him breathing but at least he wasn't attacking. I threw the sleeping bags down to Healey and then handed him the Johnson rifle in its sheepskin-lined case. Just as I was about to swing myself out, with the pistol tucked into my belt, the carcajou attacked again. He came fast and low, a dark blur, silent, and slashed me on the left knee. Then he was gone, where I could not tell. I dropped down into the snow.

"Hit you again?" Healey asked beside me. "Shit, Jack, that doesn't look so good."

"Let him have the plane," I said. "He's welcome to it. I'll give him flying lessons free of charge. By mail. But I'm not going back in there again."

It had socked in by now and there was the taste of snow on the air. We rigged the tarpaulin as a lean-to over by the rocks and cut spruce boughs to bed our sleeping bags. Then we opened the emergency kits and had lunch—corned beef hash out of the can and a can of cold peaches—and a couple of stiff belts of brandy. I'd poured sulfa powder over the wolverine slashes and bandaged them properly, but both wounds were aching badly and stiffening up. The brandy helped. It started to snow in earnest.

"There's no one going to see us," Healey said. "The goddam plane's as white as the glacier. And now with this snow . . ."

"They'll miss us in Fairbanks and they've got our flight plan." I didn't even want to think about siwashing out of that country, not with my knee chewed up. We'd been forced down before— it's part of the bush pilot's way of life, perhaps the most interesting part—but we'd always been picked up in a matter of a day or two at most. Once we'd had to put down on a gravel bar over on the coast near Dillingham in Bristol Bay. An oil leak. We patched the leak and then found we didn't have the spare oil along. But Healey went out for a hike and found a whale carcass beached not far from the plane. We hacked off some blubber and melted it down to oil over the fire, and presto! Back in business.

Another time, I was flying Charlie Hall's gullwing Stinson while he recovered from the flu, lugging the mail up to Eagle, when I spotted a nice young bull moose on the flats below me. We needed the meat, so I picked a spot well ahead of his line of travel and put down on a bar in the river. I was sitting pretty behind some down timber when the moose came by, trot-trot-trot, like he was late for a hot date in Dawson City, his neck all swollen with the rut, and I hit him pretty hard, I thought, with a round from my .303. He went down. Not thinking, I leaned my rifle against the log I'd used as a rest, and went over to butcher him out. Whoops! Up he got and came for me. I barely made it up a tree. Then he found my rifle and stomped it into a steel pretzel. Then he saw the plane. His eyes caught fire. In two minutes, he turned Charlie's pretty little red-and-black gullwing into a heap of slashed fabric and splintered struts. Then he trotted on over the horizon as if nothing had happened. I must have just creased him. At any rate, I made a cold camp and shivered until noon the next day when Healey came over looking for me in Billy Forbes's Ryan B-1. "Christ, Jack-O," he said when he landed. "After I spotted that wreckage, I figured I'd be collecting you with a soup spoon. What happened?"

"Don't ask."

So I figured we'd best just sit tight here on the glacier and wait for them to come to us. I reckoned without the carcajou. It snowed all that afternoon and most of the night. Healey gathered a big pile of deadwood and we had a hot supper and turned in early, our heavy kapok bags warm and toasty near the fire. On toward dawn, I woke to Healey screaming.

"Haaaah! Get him offa me! Get off! Eck-eck-eck. . . ."

The fire had died down and I could see him flailing around in his sleeping bag, a big black writhing fat worm in the dark there, and I grabbed the Johnson rifle and fired twice into the sky. I hoped the shots would spook the animal away.

"What is it? Bear?"

"No," Healey called back. "It was your pal from the plane. Goddam him all to hell. Oh, shit!"

He came over and threw some dry spruce on the coals and we had light. His face was ripped up and his right ear dangled black with blood. He was shaking like a whole mountainside of aspen there in the fall when the wind is working the pale leaves. I handed him the brandy bottle. He took a long gulping swig.

"Pour some of that over your ear and I'll sew it back on for you."

"Like hell," he said. "Not till I stop shaking."

We stayed up the rest of the night in front of the fire, listening to the carcajou as he went his destructive rounds. For a while he was in the cockpit, ripping up the seats and smashing the instrument panel. Then he was back out on the wing chewing on the props. Then back into the cargo deck slinging cans and tools around like a machinists' convention. He never got tired. Just wreck-wreck-wreck. Now and then, we could hear him emptying his bowels on whatever he had just smashed. Healey sat hunkered with his elbows on his knees, his face dead sober, his head bandaged over the torn ear that I'd sewn back on to the accompaniment of his constant whining and bitching. It must have hurt plenty, though, I'll give him that.

"Why doesn't he go away?" Sam Healey asked. "He's got to have wrecked everything three times over already."

"He's onto a good thing. You know old Emile Picot down there in Cordova? He can tell you about wolverines. He had a trapline up in the Wrangells one winter and a carcajou sniffed it out. Followed him around all winter and whenever he took an animal in the set, the carcajou would rip it up and eat half of it and piss on the rest. Finally, the carcajou tried to get into Emile's line cabin. But he had it boarded up tight. The carcajou came down the chimney when Emile was away and destroyed everything in the cabin—food, books, ammo, hides, table and chairs. He ripped Emile's only sleeping bag into a blizzard. No way Emile could get him, either with the rifle or in a trap. Finally, he gave up and cleared out. He went back two seasons later and the carcajou was waiting for him, ready to start all over again. So Emile went down to Ketchikan and signed on a halibut schooner and never did go trapping again."

"Carcajou," Sam said.

"It's an Algonkian Indian word, means 'devil,' hence the nickname 'Injun Devil.' Latin name *Gulo luscus*, the Glutton, the Gulper. Circumpolar distribution in mountains and northern tundra. May be same species as Old World glutton. Rare. Fortunately."

"Eats airplanes, the larger the better."

"And ears of their pilots."

"Well, one thing's for danged sure," Sam said, touching the bandaged ear, "I'm not spending another night in the same country as that guy. We're going to have to pack out of here. Siwash it."

CHAPTER FIVE

*D*AWN BROKE: a still and cloudless day. The Dakota lay half buried in new snow and the glacier rolled away in easy undulations, shadowed in its swales a pale bruise blue. We walked out toward the lip of the glacier, feeling our way cautiously with spruce poles so that we didn't inadvertently step onto a fragile snow bridge masking a crevasse. My knee was stiff at first, but it loosened with the walking. Still, I didn't know how much strain it could take over the long haul. At the lip of the glacier, the ice began to crackle and the crevasses grew too wide for leaping. We went back up the shoulder of the mountain that flanked the glacier. The country on the far side was all tumbledown cliffs and sharp unitaks. From the shoulder, we could look out over the country we'd have to traverse if we were to get out of that place.

I didn't know it at the time, of course, but I was taking my first look at the country where I would make my life. It was a place where I would be happier than anywhere else in the world, and sadder. And, finally, angrier—country that would pit Healey against me in a bitter bloody duel from which only one of us could possibly emerge alive. Even with that final battle imminent, with thirty years behind us and our friendship gone rancid with his greed, I cannot truly hate him. But I must. . . .

The snout of the glacier, blue and pocked and studded with boulders, fell off nearly sheer for five hundred feet to the widening valley below. The country down there looked rusty green, smooth as a meadow, spotted here and there with glacier-scoured rock outcroppings splashed bright with lichen and moss. Two rivers snaked through the valley: one, milky white with glacial melt, feeding out of the ice itself, the other cutting down from the ridges to the north, clear and frothing only over its rapids. Black and yellow trees lined the rivers and their feeder streams, and big stands of spruce dotted the valley. Small lakes and potholes flashed like mirrors in the early light. Away off to the west, beyond a black line of coastal rain forest, you could see the hard blue-black line of the Gulf of Alaska.

"It looks like a golf course," Sam said happily. "A million-hole golf course."

"I make it about forty or fifty miles to the coast," I said. "That's a long hike. And you know damned well that what looks like a golf course from up here will turn out to be muskeg down there."

Still, it was magnificent country and, despite my knee, I wanted to walk it. We went back to the plane and got our gear together, packing what we could fit into two musette bags. First aid kit, lighter fluid and smokes, Geodetic Survey charts of the region, a Boy Scout compass, some Gillette Blue Blades, six Hershey bars with almonds, the rest of our brandy and all the canned goods we could cram in. The tarp would be too heavy for one man to carry alone, so we haggled it apart with a pocket knife and each took half. I planned to carry the Johnson and gave Sam the .45.

"We could use some rope going down that cliff," he said.

"There's a coil of manila just back of the cockpit door in the hold," I told him. "Why don't you go in there and get it? Maybe you can pay back our furry friend for the ear."

"Like hell." Then he thought for a bit, looking warily at the plane. We hadn't heard the carcajou since first light. "Maybe he's gone. Maybe he heard his mother calling." He steeled himself and went over to the plane, waited a long minute, then began climbing the spruce snag ladder into the cockpit. I watched him lean in cautiously, turn his head from side to side, then slide in farther as he reached for the coil of rope. I had the Johnson up and ready in case the wolverine showed, either in the cockpit or at the cargo door.

"Cripes!"

He exploded out the window like a champagne cork, the coil of rope snaking in his left hand. The spruce tree leaned out and away from its rest against the nose of the Dakota and for a long, teetering moment Healey balanced up there, a frozen pole vaulter, swaying back and forth. Then the tree fell backward to the ground. I could see the carcajou stick his flat ugly head out the window, eyes flashing evil, but before I could lay the rifle sights on him, he was gone.

"Did he get you?"

"No, thank God. But I think the only reason he missed was that he was back in there packing." Sam brushed the snow from his sleeves and gestured with the rope coil. "Got the manila, though. That's something. Why didn't you shoot when he stuck his head out?"

"I'm getting to kind of like him. He's a laugh a minute. You up there on that pole—it was better than a circus."

It took the rest of that day just to get down the side of the mountain. Some of the time, we waded armpit deep in soft melting snow. At other times, we had to line our way down steep faces rather than go the long, slow way around. My knee was beginning to throb and I wrapped it tight in a hunk of canvas from the tarp, but then it was too stiff to flex properly so I took the canvas off. The flesh around the fang holes was red and puffy, with crusts of pale green pus showing. I scraped the pus away and sprinkled on more sulfa. But puncture wounds don't hold sulfa like a good clean slash. It ached deep down in there.

We drank glacial melt from the cans we had opened for our dinner, cold and gritty from the ice-ground rock the glacier had been polishing for the last ten thousand years. We watched our backtrail closely, but saw no sign of the carcajou. Maybe he decided to stay with the plane. It seemed a perfect playground for a lad of his bent. I *was* beginning to like that animal. What an appetite! God he was tough. In those early years I had not yet met up face to face with an angry grizzly, only a few rather phlegmatic black bears, and the carcajou was the first animal I had encountered (other than man) that ran both ways—toward you more often than not. There was something very deep and basic in the tingle you felt when you saw an animal coming your way with malice on its breath. Not a pleasant feeling, to be sure, but certainly a stirring one. I'm half convinced that he could dodge bullets. I've seen ducks, particularly green-wing teal, roll away from a pattern of chilled birdshot, eyes on mine as they pass, then folding one wing and executing a perfect barrel roll as they drop under the shot. The carcajou seemed able, even in the dark, to watch the bullet emerge from the gunbarrel and simply to step aside, letting it pass as a matador would a charging bull.

The sun was sinking fast toward the Gulf when we finally reached bottom. It was warmer in the valley than up on the ice, but not by much. My knee was about finished so we decided to make camp beside the clear river that flowed in from the northern scarp. Where the two streams met the milky glacial runoff and the clear water surged and swirled together, the clear current pulling clouds and tendrils of murk into itself, gray-green puffs of spinning smoke. Long dark shadows moved in and out of the murk and I caught a flash of red as one of the fish rolled—a big cutthroat trout, feeding along the edge between dark and light. Skulls and vertebrae of last summer's salmon run littered the bank, and where it dipped to a natural ford we saw fresh moose sign, the big pad marks of a brown bear and the pockings of many caribou. Up on the ridge flanking the glacier we had seen sheep droppings. This was a rich country.

Healey came out of a spruce thicket dragging two blowdowns for the fire. "There's a bog back in there that smells of oil," he said. He scraped black muck off his boots and sniffed it. "Take a whiff."

"Probably oozing out from under the glacier," I said. "There's a big seepage like that under the Valdez glacier but the oil companies aren't interested. Too difficult to extract, they say. There's probably oil all through this country, but it's too damn tough to get it out. Gold is easier. Gold and fur and timber. The big treasure in this valley is the game. You could build a lodge right here where the two rivers meet and have top flyfishing within walking distance. If you worked the country carefully and weren't too greedy, you'd never shoot all the game out. The caribou come through, like it or not. Keep the wolves in check and the moose would prosper. You might want to thin out the bears some. No sense having your clients chewed up."

"Yeah, and that carcajou."

"You could put in a string of spike camps up in the mountains and go after the Dall sheep in season. You could range out all through these mountains and set up a circuit of semi-permanent camps, rotating them over the years so that you'd never put too much pressure on any one hunk of country. You could do it forever."

Lying in our bags around the fire that night, sipping Labrador tea spiked with brandy, we talked about our hunting lodge. In those days you could still homestead in that section of Alaska. All you had to do was improve the property by five hundred dollars over a three-year period. We could do that just by putting up a small cabin. A small cabin to start, but then expanding it, doing it right: a big, high-ceilinged main room with a stand-up English-style stone fireplace and a lot of heads on the walls; rocking chairs built of caribou racks with lacquered snowshoe webbing; bearskin rugs and bearskins on the beds in the guest rooms; a separate room for a library like we'd seen in the big old houses in India from the days of the Raj. One thing we'd learned in Alaska, felt it ourselves, was a hunger for books. The farther north you go in this world, and the deeper you penetrate the wild places, the more literate the people who live there. Apart from the radio—which was used as much for gossip as it was for legitimate emergencies—there was no other way to stay in touch with the rest of the world. Not that Alaskans would like to be living in the Outside, but rather that learning of the Outside's latest acts of arrant idiocy gave them a sense of superiority. Another odd thing: living lives of high adventure, they craved more than ever the spurious adventures of others, as filtered through the written word. A woman alone in a log cabin on a remote mountain hours from any other human being might take out the compost pail one morning and find a brown bear standing in her vegetable garden. She would go back into the house, take the Remington .338 Magnum off the wall, step outside, kill the bear with a brain shot, and then pour a cup of coffee and return to *The Sweet Cheat Gone.*

But the situation was ideal for a hunting lodge. It was far enough inland to be spared the incessant drenching rains of the coast. There was enough spruce and willow to heat with wood year around, plenty of water. Not so boggy that mosquitoes would drive you out, though they are a perennial pest everywhere in the summertime north—mosquitoes and black flies and no-see-ums so thick in all these parts that I've seen caribou dead with their nostrils plugged with matted black insect bodies, seen moose go crazy and crash off cliffs from the fly bites. But by the time the hunting season rolled around late in August, the flying insects had usually vanished, frozen out by early frosts. It would be perfect.

"Let's file on it," Healey said. "A damn good investment. If the game ever ran out, we could always tap the oil."

We both laughed at that. In those days, oil was the cheapest commodity in the world. Or so it seemed.

CHAPTER SIX

AND SO we left the country that the carcajou had showed us—"The Valley of the Devil," as Healey called it. We built a raft of dried spruce logs, burning them to size in the campfire and lashing them together with the manila line. According to our charts, we were on the headwaters of the Alugiak River. Before we broke camp, we placed cairns at the corners of the section we planned to homestead, estimating the acreage as best we could from our detail chart and leaving our names and the date, written on pages torn from the flight log, buried in taped tin cans under the stones. Later, we could run a more precise survey.

The weather held fair and we made good time, drifting silently on the strong green current with the sky a high hard blue overhead filled with the piercing dog yap of migrating geese. Around nearly every bend, we flushed rafts of ducks and geese off the slow water of the back eddies. I killed one with a lucky head shot from the Johnson, a young snow goose just at the start of its takeoff. We surprised a family of black bears, a sow and two cubs, stuffing themselves on skunk cabbage in the mucky shallows of a slough. They stood hock deep in the ooze staring vacantly at us with shredded vegetation dripping from their jaws, as if they had never seen men before. Innocents in an Arctic Eden.

We made camp that night—our last on the river, we hoped—on a broad gravel bar in an oxbow bend where the breeze would keep the mosquitoes down. As the weather warmed, they had appeared in clouds, forcing us to midstream to avoid them. But as the sun sloped lower and the shadows lengthened along the banks, a chill knifed into the air and the mosquitoes began to disappear. Even in midsummer, with the sun shining nearly twenty-four hours, ice is never far beneath the surface. It is always cold in the shadows.

We roasted the goose over a slow fire, catching the fat drippings in the concave surface of a flat, ice-hollowed stone. After two days of canned goods and a lot of labor, we were ravenous. I found a stand of Indian rice—a chocolate-flowered iris-like plant with small edible bulbs—growing in a meadow back of the gravel bar and we roasted the bulbs on another rock at the side of the fire, seasoning them with wild chives. The aroma of our cooking was almost unbearable as we waited for the goose to be done. I wondered if I looked as beat out as Healey. He lay propped on one elbow beside the fire, his face and hands lumpy with bug bites, the bandage over his torn ear spotted yellow-brown where it had leaked. My own injured knee was swollen to twice its normal size. Lining the raft down the last set of rapids, I had slipped and smashed it against a sharp boulder. Despite the fire, my bones still ached from immersion in the cold ice-fed water.

Yet for all our aches and bruises, for all that our sole means of livelihood lay smashed on top of the glacier far behind us, for all that we did not know what the night, much less tomorrow, would bring us in the way of trial and fresh peril, we were happier, there in front of that sputtering fire on that chilly windswept gravel bar, than we had ever been before. We were young then, and strong, and certainly naive. But this was what had brought us to Alaska: the challenge of strong country, the chance to pit our strength and skill against something stronger, pitiless but not impersonal, a land as young and raw as we were, yet infinitely tougher. I guess we could be called masochists, for suffering in that country was a kind of privilege. Scars were our wound stripes. Walk down any muddy street in any scruffy Alaskan town and count the fingers on the men you pass. Even if they all have both their arms, you'll be lucky to count ninety on the first ten you see. Empty eyesockets, peg legs, burn scars and axe scars: Badges of Honor.

Something splashed in the darkness of the river. Healey glanced over at the holstered .45 and unsnapped the safety flap. The glint of firelight on wood.

"Hello the camp! May I come ashore?"

The man who dragged the heavily laden freight canoe up onto the shingle was short and squareshouldered in a faded red wool shirt and stagged corduroy pants tucked into the top of high lace-up mukluks. His long white hair was held back from his forehead by a wide rawhide sweatband. Bright black eyes, wide cheekbones, a short hooked nose, heavy jaw, wide mouth. An Indian.

"I'm Jack Slade and this is my partner, Sam Healey. We'd offer you some coffee but we haven't got any. But you're welcome to some goose if you're hungry."

"Thank you, thank you," the old man said. He spoke as if he were still hailing us from the middle of the river. In a windstorm. "Just dropped in to see if you were all right. I'm Charlie Blue, ha-ha. Old Charlie Blue. Been here forever. Last Tlingit on the river. Ha-ha. When I was a boy, the glacier stuck its snout in the sea, like a great blue elephant sucking salt water. The mountains spouted fire and smoke. Wolves as big as horses. Giant icebergs. Schools of whales so thick you could spear them from the beach. Plenty to eat. Big timber for ancestor houses. War with the Haida. War with the Eskimos. Then the Russians came with their Aleut slaves and lied and stole our furs and tried to whip us with their big heavy whips but we pushed them into the river and killed them. Yes, thank you, I am hungry. You boys in trouble?"

Healey sliced him a slab of dark, fat-dripping breast meat and the old Indian stuffed it in his mouth, his heavy jaws working and fat dripping off his chin. While he was chewing, I told him about the plane.

"Oh, that's marvelous!" he laughed, wiping his chin and

licking his fingers. "Carcajou ate you right out of the sky! My goodness, he must have been hungry to eat an airplane. Oh my! Splendid! May I have some more of that excellent goose meat? Thank you, thank you."

Between chomps and swallows, he raved on and on about the appetite of the carcajou, seemingly growing hungrier at every mouthful, every exclamation. In five minutes, he had eaten three quarters of the goose and the greater share of the roasted iris bulbs. Then he belched and fixed his eye on the brandy bottle, which stood half empty beside the packs. I uncorked it and passed it over. He began to gulp and the level fell, fell, until there was perhaps an inch left. He belched again and then finished it off, like so much water.

"Ah, that was fine! That was splendid! But I must be going now. Going up into the country. Have a look around. See how things are up there. Do you have any salt you could spare? Any sugar? How about bullets—.22 and .303? No. Too bad. Toilet paper? Matches? No. I see you have almost nothing. The carcajou left you nothing. Well, here—take this." He pulled a necklace of bearclaws off from around his thick, wrinkled neck and handed it to me. "It's magic," he whispered, looking around into the darkness. "It will take you where you want to go, make everything all right." He got up lithely for a man of his years and walked back to the canoe. Healey and I helped him shove off and we saw him turn out of the light and dig in for the upstream haul. "Ha-ha!" We could hear him laughing as he disappeared into the rushing darkness. "Carcajou! That was splendid! Marvelous!"

For a long while we could hear him laughing and yelling to himself.

"Some old man," Sam said wryly. He rattled the bearclaws. "Did you see him scoff that goose? Did you see him chug that brandy? I know you're supposed to share when you meet strangers in the bush, but that's carrying it a bit too far, wouldn't you say?"

When we got back to the fire, the goose was sputtering fat as ever, whole and high, over the fire. The brandy bottle stood full beside the packs. A sharp-bitted cruising axe leaned against the hunk of driftwood I had been using as a backrest, its edge gleaming in the light of the flames.

"What the hell?" Sam said. "Sleight of hand?"

"He's a shaman," I said. "In this country anything's possible."

The next morning, we were awakened by the sound of an airplane engine. It was Wally Mayhew's Fairchild 71. He spotted us and wagged his wings, then put down on the river and taxied over to the gravel bar. He leaned out with a big grin on his freckled face. "Where the hell you guys been? I been looking all over the place for you."

When we told him, hesitantly, about our visitor of the previous evening and his little bit of food wizardry, Wally looked at us very closely, then looked away. "You guys are bushwhacky, that's all." We let it go at that.

A few hours later, we were in Gurry Bay making plans to fly back to the glacier, rig the Dakota out with skis, repair the damage and fly her off.

The carcajou was gone when we returned.

CHAPTER SEVEN

LATER, CHARLIE Blue told me more about the war between the Tlingit and Mother Russia.

The leader of the Russian expedition was one Vassily Sergeevich Volkov, a captain in Aleksandr Baranov's Russian-America Company, which administered Russian Alaska prior to the U.S. purchase in 1867. When the purchase was agreed to, the company's directors ordered all captains to mount a final assault on the wealth of the country. Head deep into the interior and take as much in the way of furs, gold and copper as they could find, extort or steal. "God is on high and the Tsar is far away."

Volkov was a man of parts. A contemporary of Tolstoi's, he served in the Caucasus campaigns and was twice mentioned in dispatches during the fighting around Inkerman during the Crimean War of the early 1850s. He was a concert-caliber violinist, a dedicated entomologist (he described fifteen new species of wood beetle during his five years in Russian America), a womanizer and duelist (won all three of them; two pistol, one saber). He was forty-two years old when he set out at the head of a party of Russians and Aleuts to rape the Alugiak. Blue says he was a short, wiry man with a wolf-gray beard halfway down his pouterpigeon chest, steely blue eyes, close set, and a saber scar on his forehead that gave him a perpetual frown. He spoke Tlingit and Aleut fluently, with scarcely a trace of an accent.

The raiding party, some fifty men strong, embarked up the river from Gurry Bay (then Nova Polyana) in five whaleboats soon after breakup in the spring of that year. Ice floes and small bergs calved from the Alugiak glacier still clogged the river as they lined their way up the big rapids just inland from the trading post. It took them a week to reach the first Tlingit camp, where the men had just finished drying their winter catch of beaver, marten, mink and ermine. Volkov offered salt and blankets for the furs. When the Tlingit refused, he had his men hold them at musket point while he personally lashed the leader to death with a knout, the long, heavy bullwhip the Russians favored in putting the fear of the Tsar into their subjects.

As the Indian breathed his last, a raven emerged from his gaping mouth and flew unharmed through a whistling barrage of Russian musket balls, heading upriver. The other Tlingit smiled, knowing this was the soul of their dead leader, flying to warn the people at the larger village up near the glacier. Seeing their smiles, Volkov ordered them shot. They laughed as the Russians charged their muskets, not trying to flee or overpower their captors, and bared their chests to the bullets. When the smoke cleared, all ten Indians lay dead on the gravel with smiles still on their faces.

The Aleuts were frightened by this display of courage and wanted to turn back, but Volkov told them to shut up or they would follow the Tlingit to the spirit world, where no doubt they would pay for their loyalty to the Russians by suffering fearful torture for all eternity. The party resumed its upriver voyage, sending scouts ahead to insure against a Tlingit ambush. The weather turned to winter again. In the mornings, the edges and back eddies of the Alugiak were coated with thin, rubbery ice. Ice crusted the muskegs and meadow grass, making it impossible for the party's hunters to approach game within killing range. Freezing rains fell day and night, and their cookfires gave off no heat. Even the furs which they had taken from the Tlingit seemed to provide no warmth, nor did the normally fiery plum brandy the officers drank. One afternoon, the sky lowering with icy clouds that whipped and snapped eerily overhead, they paused at the foot of a rapids to plot their ascent. Suddenly, a huge ice floe came crashing over the falls, crushing two boats together against the rocky bank. The boats splintered, foundered and sank, taking twenty of their party with them.

Candlefish were running upriver to spawn, a variety of smelt that is the first anadromous fish to appear in Alaskan streams each year: the eulachon or "hooligan" of the literature. They are so full of fat that one can literally light them, once they have dried a few hours, and use them for illumination. The Aleuts netted hundreds, planning to glut themselves on the fat and regain some of their strength, but these candlefish were so rancid that those who ate them vomited them back up in minutes.

That night, a great blue glacier bear came bowling into camp and killed four Aleuts along with a young Russian officer named Chernovsky. It carried Chernovsky off into the spruce thicket and all night they heard him screaming. In the morning, as the sun rose behind a dirty gray band of sky back of the black spruces, they saw the young Russian's head stuck on a pikestaff in the bow of Volkov's very own pinnace. A raven was perched on Chernovsky's head, making a breakfast of his eyes. The raven gurgled and laughed, then flew insolently over their heads with an eyeball dangling blue and tendrilous from its heavy black beak. Tears dropped from the Russian's eye, and where they touched the glacier-scoured rock, stalagmites grew.

Now two of the oldest Aleuts, named Vinkov and Maranovich, approached Vassily Sergeevich and pleaded with him to return to Nova Polyana. The expedition was under some awful curse. Their bullets had passed through the glacier bear without drawing blood. The ice was thickening by the hour. The sky to the north promised snow—heavy, wet, clinging snow that would freeze at night into a burial shroud. These men were trusted servants of the Company who had worked all their lives for the Russians with never a moment's complaint, much less any sign of cowardice. Volkov placed his hands on their shoulders and reassured them.

"This is how it must be, my sons," he said (though he was twenty years younger than either of them). "In life, if one turns back from action just once, he will turn back again and again. We will find food and warmth and women at the glacier camp. We will find more furs than we can carry in our boats. We may well find gold and copper, enough so that all of you can leave our service and return to Adak, spend the rest of your lives around the stove tending the samovar. Have heart. We are nearly there."

They continued upriver through the snow, which fell in large wet flakes so thickly and silently that it was as if they were moving, heavy limbed, through the gauze of nightmare. Volkov stood in the bow of the lead boat playing cheerful airs on his violin. But the men—Russian and Aleut alike—felt only dread. Toward evening, the snow stopped falling and the sky grew clear. The country all around them lay blanketed in white and ahead of them they saw the sapphire glitter of the late falling sun on the glacier's face. But despite the sun, despite their fur garments, despite their strenuous exertions at the oars, the men felt colder than ever. Their teeth chattered and their bones ached with the chill. Then they saw columns of smoke rising blue and thin behind a grove of bare aspens that fringed the river.

"There it is, my children," exulted Volkov. "The village of the Tlingit! Now we will work our vengeance upon them."

They beached the surviving whaleboats on the gravel bar. The aspen grove masked them from the village. Volkov's plan was to move quietly through the trees and then, on a signal, open fire into the village, following up with a charge using axes and sabers. The glacier towered over them as they filtered through the pale, yellow-green boles of the aspens, a great rough wall of blue ice studded with sharp snags of broken granite. Their muskets primed and freshly capped, their sidearms checked and ready, they neared the end of the thicket. Peering out, they saw a sight that froze what was left of their marrow.

Instead of an Indian camp, they saw twenty-five tall salmon

racks, of the sort the Tlingit use to smoke their summer catch. As in a nightmare, they saw *themselves* spreadeagled on the racks, mouths working in mad but silent agony, naked, their skins bursting and bubbling to the slow heat of the aspenwood fires that smoked and licked beneath them. Volkov himself hung from the centermost rack. His beard smoldered. His violin, lying atop the hot coals, crackled and burst into flame, its strings popping in an eerie, electric singsong.

A raven flapped slowly overhead, its bright black eye gazing down at them. As it passed under the glowering blue face of the glacier, it uttered a single harsh, high scream.

The glacier grumbled and groaned, a deep rending scream echoing that of the raven. A single tall serac at dead center of the ice face creaked and toppled, slowly, to crash in an explosion of ice on the rocks below. Then the glacier opened. A mammoth gusher of milk-blue water roared out of the ice, water that had accumulated behind the frozen dam for years, cascading down on the men with a grinding, grating rush, carrying ice and boulders and trees and the bodies of long-dead animals with it.

By dawn the next day, the breakout had dwindled to a trickle. The gravel beach lay bare and glistening under the first rays of the sun. Yakataga Charlie, the Tlingit shaman, found Volkov's body bent and twisted in a tangle of timbers a mile downstream. He removed the Russian's head and smoked it over a slow fire until the skin was cured a dark brown and the eyeballs sunk back into the skull like withered black olives. The skull hung in his lodge for many years afterward.

CHAPTER EIGHT

GURRY BAY wasn't much of a town back then, not even by Alaskan standards. There was the cannery, the sawmill, Hank Maynard's boatyard and gas station; the Gurry Bay Mercantile & Fur Emporium and the Blue Bear Saloon, both owned by Norman Ormandy; a scattering of shanties, house trailers and log cabins, and the town dump at the end of the Airport Road that ran out east through the spruce flats toward the far, white mountains. Except for what folks called "the raddio," the only entertainment of a nonalcoholic or nonviolent nature was visiting the dump of an evening to watch the brown bears feed and feud through the garbage. There was no road to Gurry Bay from the Outside in those days; you got there by boat or plane or you didn't get there at all, not that you'd miss it.

For most of the year, the cannery, which was owned by a Kodiak outfit, stood empty and echoing. Small boys would drop by to shoot the rats that swarmed in the pilings where the salmon boats tied up to offload during the season. The ping of .22s snapped and echoed along the empty piers and the rats chittered in panic, dragging their naked tails through the slime. The cannery came alive only during the two-month summer run. We would fly a crew in from Kodiak—a handful of tough, hard-driving supervisors, Swedes mainly, and a scruffy gang of working stiffs: boozy Aleuts and Aleut–Russkies, hard-eyed knife-happy river eskimos from the Kuskokwim country, stumblebums from Skid Row in Seattle (or "Skedaddle," as we called it) and a goodly number of cleancut college kids and schoolteachers from Outside who came up during their summer vacations for the high wages. Many of this last group quit early because of the long, hard drudgery of the lines and the incessant violence of their off hours.

During these months, at least, the town hummed. Millions of bright fish, fresh from the salt chuck, many with the sea lice still on them, poured out of the seiners' holds and into the belching, chugging maw of the cannery: humpies and dogs, silvers and reds and a handful of giant black-speckled gate-mouthed kings. The whole town and the woods and ocean for miles around took on a sweet-sour reek of gurry—the gluey salmon slime that gave the town its name.

The Tlingit in this area believed that salmon gurry was akin to the secretions of a sexually aroused woman, and to be sure during the salmon season the whole town smelled like a rumpled bed at the bitter end of love. Maybe the energy of the spawning salmon had something to do with it as well, but during the season the town throbbed thick-necked with the rutting instinct. There was love in the morning, love in the afternoon: couples balling upright in alleyways, or sprawled writhing and moaning on mossy blowdowns rotting back into the rainforest floor, or guys walking away slackhipped down the dock with goofy grins on their faces, their knees and elbows rubbed raw by their exertions on a pile of salt-dried salmon web.

And along with the balling, of course, came the brawling. There were bar fights and street fights, fist fights and knife fights, and occasionally something serious (i.e., involving a wife) that called for the use of firearms. When you consider that even a half-blind Alaskan woman with palsy can shoot the eyes off a Marine Corps marksman at fifty paces, it's amazing that more of the gunfights didn't end with someone flaked out in the cannery ice house. There were, however, no end of perforated kneecaps and plenty of guys who emerged from the infirmary talking in a higher register.

The unofficial town hall and social center, though, was the Blue Bear Inn and its adjunct, the Mercantile & Fur Emporium. Both were housed in the long, low-roofed building that once served as the Russian-America Company's trading post and manufactory, a structure built of thick logs that looked furry with the moss of a century. The roof, in that wet climate, supported an ecosystem of its own, moss and lichens, and in the spring and summer wildflowers bloomed up there, low-bush cranberries bore fruit, and every few years, Norman Ormandy and his companion, a Salish halfbreed named LaFourche, would have to climb up with saws and pruning shears to remove the spruce and cedar whips whose roots threatened to invade the interior. For a number of years, a family of willow ptarmigan nested each spring near the stove-pipe that came up from the kitchen. Emerging drunk and fragile in the dawn, possessed by that hollow feeling that anything is possible and nothing real, one would hear the chicks peeping and wonder if it was just the final, long-anticipated cerebral collapse, come at last.

Though the Blue Bear was situated on a spit of land that afforded a splendid view of the Alugiak Falls and the vast blue reach of the Gulf of Alaska, there was not a window in the place. Once, when we were new in town, I asked Ormandy why.

"Take a look," he said, gesturing toward the gang of wool-shirted, hip-booted men and women hunched happily at the long mahogany bar. "They're out in it all day. Lumberjacks, Cat skinners, salmon seiners, prospectors, trappers, Indians, cannery stiffs. Once they're finished work, they don't want to see the son of a bitch. If you worked in a factory Outside, would you want a picture window in your living room that looked right into the assembly line?"

The only reminder of the wilderness surrounding Gurry Bay, out beyond those mossy walls, was the full body mount of a blue-furred glacier bear that stood near the door, erect and awful with its jaws agape and its paws extended in the time-honored threat of the bear hug. Someone had hung a sign in the shape of a cartoonist's balloon from the bear's jaws. It read, "C'mon, honey, give us a little smooch." Blue bears were just color variations on the common black bear, adapted to glacier country, not as aggressive as grizzlies or coastal browns, but tough enough anyway. They were unique to this stretch of the Alaskan coast. Norman liked to shadowbox with the bear, dancing around like Willie Pep, flicking jabs at the bear's silent, snarling jaw and then crossing hard with his right to the ribcage—*thwock*!

"You ought to come up into the country with me sometime and try that on a bear that can punch back," I told him.

"No thanks. I like it here just fine."

Most of the men in town went out into the bush only with the greatest of reluctance, and then only to make their winter meat. Moose was the staple of their winter diet and in those days, before wolves were protected from aerial hunting, which was the only efficient way to cull them, there were plenty of moose to go around. A single moose provided meat enough for a family of six to make it through the winter—some five hundred pounds of it—though after a few months of nothing but moose steak, mooseburger, braised moose nose au gratin, moose stew and moose croquettes, it began to pall.

No, the clientele of the Blue Bear preferred to sit around the bar every evening after work, bitching or bragging about how rough it had been that day out there, listening to Hank Williams or Eddie Arnold on the juke, and getting pie-eyed on drinks they invented from the bottles that stood under the mirror behind the bar. A "Williwaw" was half beer, half Irish whiskey, with a dollop of horseradish for zest. An "Irish Nigger" was crème de menthe and crème de cacao, over ice. Most potent of all was the infamous "Red Brick" (or "Red Prick," as some styled it)—a mixture of sloe gin, bitters, vodka and tequila topped off with a maraschino cherry and a slice of lime. One of them excised your kneecaps. Two spelled Puke City.

I like to drink as much as the next man, but in the Blue Bear the drinking had an ugly, hysterical undertone to it much of the time, a sour stench of ennui and defeat and bottled rage waiting to erupt. A constipation of the soul that only blood could clear, only suicide or murder.

When I got back from filing our homestead papers in Juneau, the salmon run was at its peak. Healey had stayed in Gurry Bay to clear up some paper work and negotiate the purchase of a Cessna 180 that we planned to convert to floats and skis for our hunting lodge. I found him in the Blue Bear, drinking with Marie Olds, and I knew we were in trouble. He was into his Clark Gable routine with a vengeance, all slow lopsided grins and merry twinkles, his deep voice husky with booze and implicit promises and his heavy shoulders hunched slightly like a man about to spring. The ear that the carcajou had chomped was nearly healed, but now it didn't jug out as far as the other, giving him a slightly rakish tilt. Marie was eating it all up with a rusty spoon. She was a big blonde gal, good looking as Alaska women go, but somewhat coarse featured. Dumb as they come, but with big knockers and a well-packed can that bulged her slacks like a couple of king salmon kissing.

The only trouble was that Marie was married. Her husband, Gainey Olds, was captain of a purse seiner (the *Sweet Marie*) and one of the meanest, most vengeful men up and down that mean and vengeful coast. Two seasons earlier, when a college kid who was crewing for him gave him some backchat, Gainey stranded the kid on a rock in the Shelikof Strait off Afognak and left him alone with the sea lions for the better part of a week. When he came back, the kid had jumped his trolley and only talked in seal yaps. Another time, he socked a salmon gaff into the buns of a cannery boss he suspected of making eyes at Marie. The cannery took him to court, but Gainey was too valuable a highliner for them to alienate, so they dropped the charges and fined him his bonus for that season. Most of the year they lived down in Ketchikan, but during the run Marie worked in the cannery where Gainey could keep an eye on her when he was in port. Gurry Bay was too small a town for her to run around without him knowing about it, so I was surprised to see her playing Sam's game.

"Jack-O my boy," said Sam. "You get it filed okay? Have a drink. Have a couple of drinks. Hey, Norman, bring this Jack-Off a double O.P. straight up. Bring us a couple too, hey Marie?" "O.P." was overproof rum from the Yukon, 160 proof and strong enough to fuel a ram jet.

Healey was flying all right.

"Sam's been telling me about your place up on the Alugiak," Marie said. "It sounds neat. Sam says as soon as the Cessna's ready, he's going to fly me up there and show me the glacier and we'll go fishing and hunting and everything."

Sam smiled his crooked grin at me and winked.

"You think Gainey will let you?" I asked her.

"Gainey and me are through," she said, pouting a bit. "I've taken enough from that palooka. The other night they came in with a load and he started yelling at me, that I was fooling around and I never foolt around, not so's he'd notice, a girl can't have no fun anymore, and he slapped me around, and I gave him the old heave-ho." I could just see that. Marie's a big girl and she packs a wallop—I once saw her cool a college asshole who got fresh with her on the packing line—but Gainey weighs about two-sixty, all of it bile and rocks. A big black hairy son of a bitch, that Gainey.

"You made the deal on the Cessna?"

"Yeah," Sam said. "I got the price we wanted and she's down at Maynard's right now. Hank's hanging the floats on her. We should be able to fly her by this weekend."

"Come on over here," I said.

We walked over to the door by the mount of the glacier bear that Norman had standing there, its paws out so that the afternoon light shone through the long, curved yellow claws.

"You're not taking her up there, are you?"

"Why not?"

"Gainey will kill you, that's why not. I don't care if she's given him the air or what. That fucker will have your balls for breakfast."

"See this?" He pulled back the flap of the flight jacket and I saw the curved walnut grip of a revolver tucked into his belt. "It's one of those new .357 Mag Colts we were reading about. I bought it off the guy who sold us the plane. He said he stopped a brown bear with it over on Kodiak. One shot."

I looked at him, then shook my head.

"You're serious. Listen, Sam, when was a coozie like that worth killing a guy over? This isn't the goddam Gold Rush anymore. You plug him and they'll have you down in the hoosegow in Sitka before you know it. There's lots of chippies better than that over on Kodiak. Why don't you save yourself the grief and fly down there for a while?"

"Now *you're* serious." He laughed, but it was tight, not that gritty Gable laugh of his. "Where's your spirit of adventure, Jack-O? Where's the old Find-'Em-Feel-'Em-Fuck-'em-and-Forget-'em Jack-Off of the good old days? The old Four-F? You're turning into a prissy old fart, partner." He laughed again and clapped me on the shoulder, then went back to the bar. He patted Marie on the butt and nuzzled her ear, then winked at me and drank.

CHAPTER NINE

I *WENT OUT* and down the boardwalk to the docks where some cannery workers were handlining for ling cod. Herring gulls squawked and circled against the pink sky. It was one of those summer evenings when the air is just going crisp and the smell of kelp feels like iodine on a nick in your soul. The sun just hangs up in the western sky, motionless, like it will never fall, and the white night goes on and on. One of the workers fishing was a girl, a young woman actually, and I sat on a bitt and watched her fish. She had her line coiled around an empty tin can and when she wound up to throw the baited hook and sinkers, her shoulder action was like that of a man. She was tall and willowy, though, with long dark hair and when she turned toward me, I could see she was pretty, in a long-nosed Egyptian kind of a way. She held her lower lip in her teeth when she threw, and the bait sailed out against the pink sky, exciting the herring gulls so that they dove toward it, but the bait splashed and sank before they could grab it. The line paid off the tin can the way it does off the spool of a spinning reel. She knew what she was doing. Then she turned and caught me looking at her. Her eyes were wideset and gray-green in that light. For a moment, we stared at each other. I wanted to smile, but I couldn't. Then she broke the gaze and looked back to her line. She folded her free arm across her chest. Not much there compared to Marie, but enough. She wore dungarees and a faded blue workshirt, but she had class.

The bell in the cannery mess hall rang last call and I walked up there and had a salmon steak, mashed potatoes and peas. It's amazing how fast salmon can pall when you eat it six days a week. I read somewhere that back in colonial times one of the New England states—Massachusetts, I think—passed a law that indentured servants should not have to eat salmon more than three times a week. Do-gooders. You'd never get a bill like that through the Alaska legislature, not even back then when salmon were so thick during the run that you couldn't see the bottoms of the rivers for their black backs.

As I was finishing my coffee, the girl from the dock came in with two others. I watched her again and this time, when she caught my eye, she nodded. I tipped my hat. Healey would have walked right over to their table and sat down with his mouth at full revs, spinning them some yarn about the mating habits of the polar bears at Kotzebue or cannibalism in the Klondike during the Rush, something that would have them all agog and off-balance. Then he would squire the girl of his choice back to our shanty on River Street and have his way with her. I never could operate that way. For me, it had to be a formal dance, agonizing, glancing eye contact, nods and half smiles, finally a few cool words, the careful painful search for precisely the right pretext to ask her "out." Whatever that meant up here. "Out" was just about all of Alaska, but it wasn't the sort of "out" you ask most girls to.

"Uh, how'd you like to go out to the dump tonight and watch the bears?"

I took my tray back to the kitchen. Ole Bengtsson, the cook, was leaning on the counter smoking one of his El Ropos and sipping coffee spiked with rum. He was the only greasy square-head I've ever met. The story goes that once a new foreman came to the cannery and insisted on inspecting the kitchen before taking over from his predecessor. Ole was making hamburgers that evening—the one meat meal of the week—and his method of shaping the patties was simplicity itself. Standing there in the steamy galley, wearing a sleeveless undershirt that only half covered his hairy gut, he would grab a hunk of hamburger, slap it under his armpit, and, sqoosh, down would come the arm, and the meat was not only shaped but salted. Machinelike. The new foreman had gulped queasily and looked at the man he was replacing. "That's nothing," the other guy had said. "You oughta see him make doughnuts."

I asked him about the girl from the dock.

"*That* twist," he snorted, scattering ashes over tomorrow's potato salad. "She's a new one, came in while you guys were away. From the Outside. They call her Josey or Joey, something like that. The bitch come in here the other day and complained about 'foreign matter' in the meatloaf. I look her up and down, see, and then I say: 'What you expect when you're eating dead Jap?' That took the wind out of her sails, you bet."

When I walked past the Blue Bear I could hear music from the juke and the usual laughter, and Healey's voice right in there with them, but I went on back to the shanty. It was a bleak barebones of a place, two rickety beds covered with rough sheets and musty O.D. army surplus blankets, a rusty sink, a heating coil that we could make coffee and fry eggs on, and mildewed beaverboard walls where Healey had pinned up a couple of Vargas Girls. I lit the kerosene lamp next to my bed and flopped. I'd been living in places like this since I left the farm. First the air corps, all the empty-hearted barracks from Texas to Frisco to Hawaii to India and China, and now Alaska. All the cheap hotel rooms in places like Juneau and Fairbanks and Sitka and Nome. In Dillingham they let you sleep in the jail, free of charge.

I heard Healey and Marie come staggering down the boardwalk, their voices low and cozy, her giggling at something he said. They stopped when they saw the light in the window. He said something and they laughed again. Then they went off, probably to her room in the dormitory. She'd shoo her roomies out and they'd have their rattle. Well, screw it, I wasn't going to evacuate the room and spend the next couple of hours leaning on the bar at the Blue Bear, listening to the same shit from the same assholes that I'd heard for more nights than I care to remember. Grim and Dim, my nighttime companions. I tried to read—something by Dos Passos, I think it was, maybe *U.S.A.*—but I couldn't concentrate. These weren't my people and this town wasn't my place. Alaska was fine, but the towns were even worse than Outside. I thought of the Alugiak, up near the glacier, and how if I were there I'd be lying next to the fire, burned down by now to coals that glowed under the random cracks of warm ash, with the lights coursing overhead the way the lights move across a Wurlitzer juke box, and that high almost inaudible hum that they have when they're really surging. The salmon would be upriver by now, gone black and tattered with their journey, the males with their jaws bent so they could scarcely close them, flesh peeling from their flanks in the instant senescence of the spawning run. Everything would be at the river for free lunch. Eagles perched in the snags, fat with dead salmon, waiting for hunger to overtake them again, then down to the water to work over the spawned out body of a fish that still twitched as the eagle ripped it. Bears ambling the banks, glossy and arrogant, stinking of dead salmon so that you could smell them long before you could see them. Wolves and weasels and skunks cashing in on nature's annual bonus. That would be something to take a girl "out" to see. I wondered if—what was her name?—Josey would be interested.

The next day, we flew a load of canned salmon up to Anchorage for shipment Outside and picked up a priority cargo of machine parts for a cannery the company owned on the Nugashak. There was weather all the way. Healey was red-eyed so I handled the flying and he navigated. Neither of us mentioned Marie Olds. Then, on the way back in to Gurry Bay, he said: "*Sweet Marie*'s due in port tonight."

I didn't say anything, just flew.

"I said *Sweet Marie*'s due in."

"So what do you expect a prissy old fart to say to that?"

"Aw, hell. You're not pissed off about that, are you? I never knew you were so goddam sensitive."

"I'm not sensitive," I answered, getting hot now and knowing he was right. "I just don't want to see you get the shit kicked out of you over some dizzy broad."

"How about that time up in Kashmir?" he said. "You and

that British major's wife. Who backed you up on that one, sport? 'Pale hands I loved beside the Shalimar.' You picked a ditsy that time, pal. A goddam nympho with a husband who liked to kick ass, one of Orde Wingate's lads, a real meanie. Had you down on the verandah, playing a bongo solo on your noggin until I came up and kicked him in the kidney. How about that, Jack-O?" We both laughed thinking about it.

"Well, I'll back you on this one, don't worry," I said. "But no gun. Okay?"

"Only if I have to."

We were shooting a stick of eight-ball in the back room of the Blue Bear when Wee Willie Hinkey came in and looked around, a week's growth of beard on his weasel kisser and his sea boots still wet. Hinkey was Gainey's mate on the *Sweet Marie*. He flicked a look at us and then went back out, whistling casually with his hands in his pockets. Healey looked up from the table and winked at me.

"Here we go, partner," he said.

He was running the solids and had three balls left to go, one of them a trick downtable carom on the four-ball. He lined it up nicely, then stood up and chalked his cue. Then he bent back down and sank it clean and crisp—whap-whap, like that. The other balls were easy and he ran the table and I went out to buy him a beer. I was turning back from the bar with a beer in each hand when Olds walked through the door with Hinkey and his skiff man, Bill Wales. Olds had a splintered swab handle in his right hand.

CHAPTER TEN

"**Y**OU BEEN messing with my wife," Gainey said. He stood there big and awful in his gurry-stained yellow slicker, his face black with a pumped-up rage that couldn't quite mask his happiness. He'd been at sea for two weeks filling his hold and taking a pounding from a cold wet enemy whom he couldn't hit back. Now he was going to do some stomping of his own.

"At her own request, you might add," says Sam, cool as you please.

The Honcho in the Poncho Meets the Macho Muchacho.

"That ain't the point," says Gainey. "A man's got to take care of what's rightly his, even if it is a damn poor thing. That bitch has been nothing but grief to me since I took up with her. But I've handled that end of it already, don't you worry. I hope you like women with no teeth. They're supposed to give terrific blow jobs."

"You're a mighty wordy bastard for an outraged husband." Sam is standing there leaning on his pool cue, grinning with his teeth and looking Gainey straight in the eye. By now the loafers at the bar—mostly off-duty cannery workers—are crowded up to the door of the poolroom shuffling and hooting and licking their lips, and more of them are pouring in the front door. I could see Josey back there in the press, waiting with the rest for the action to start.

"You smart-ass flyboy," says Gainey, grinning back. "We're gonna give you back what you give Marie." He gestured with the broken-off swab handle. "We're gonna give you a good fucking over with this here stick, splinters and all, and then we're gonna nut you. Like a shoat."

About that time, Norman Ormandy comes pushing through the crowd with that sawed off ten gauge of his.

"Take it out on the dock, Gainey," he says. "I'm not having my place busted up by you goons. This isn't *The Spoilers* and I'm not Marlene Dietrich."

That got a laugh from the crowd. Norman was what in those days we called a pansy, a slim, balding, doleful man who had come into Gurry Bay before the war on the lam from a morals charge in San Francisco. Today, he would be called "gay," I guess, though how anyone so mopey could be thus classified beats me hollow. His little boyfriend, Too-Tight LaFourche, stood next to him holding the 7-mm. "Baby Nambu" automatic he claimed to have taken off a Jap marine on Attu during the Aleutian Campaign. I watched him pop rats with it one afternoon on the dock and I never doubted his story.

"What's to keep these ginks from putting the boots to me the minute we're out the door?" says Sam.

"We'll escort you," says Norman.

The whole gang troops on out of the saloon and down to the dock, cannery workers laying off bets right and left as if it were a heavyweight fight, chattering excitedly in five or six languages, hip boots flapping and feet clomping on the hollow weathered boards. The mercury-vapor lamps gave the whole scene a washed-out, hard-edged look. The tide was out and the masts of the seiners tied up alongside barely cleared the top of the dock. You could see the crabs scuttle on the mossy pilings. I caught Josey looking at me and gave her a wink, braver than I felt. She smiled back doubtfully.

The crowd formed a circle around Gainey and Sam. Gainey

handed the swab stick to Wee Willie. I stood near Willie and Bill Wales, ready to wade in if they interfered. Sam and Gainey had stripped down to their skivvy shirts and I couldn't see the pistol in Healey's belt. He was wearing Wellingtons, though, and I wondered if he had it tucked in the top of a boot. If so, his footwork was going to suffer.

Gainey moved in low, with his arms out, in a wrestler's crouch, hoping to tackle Sam and use his seventy-pound weight advantage to pin him and then demolish him with his fists. Each paw looked like it weighed ten pounds. Sam circled away and then shifted in with a left that smacked loud on Gainey's cheekbone. Gainey grunted and lunged, but Sam slipped away to his right, circling just out of range of Gainey's long grab. He caught Gainey with another left, on the ear, and then crossed a right to his eyebrow. He was still grinning, his teeth clenched, up on his toes and moving well. He couldn't have the Colt in his boot, not the way he was moving.

Gainey gave up the wrestling approach and stood straight up, aping Sam's stance and throwing a left of his own. Sam slipped it and faked a right to Gainey's kidney, then hooked his left to Gainey's mouth as Gainey came around trying to face him. It drew blood, a black smear in the vapor light. Gainey sucked it in and spat at Sam. Sam batted the glob away with his left hand.

"You're slow, Gainey," he said. "Fat and slow. You can't even spit fast."

"Bastard."

Gainey lunged in swinging with both hands and Sam backed away to the edge of the open space, circling to his right, popping and popping through Gainey's clumsy swings, and when they stopped moving the blood was running black down Gainey's upper lip and over his chin. His right eye was coming up and he was starting to breathe hard. But I could see that Sam's left fist was swollen too. You can't fight bareknuckle very long, not if you're connecting.

I looked around and I couldn't see Wee Willie. Bill Wales looked at me and shook his head as if to say he didn't want any part of this. Bill was a good gee, with a wife and four kids, and he skiffed for Gainey because he needed the money.

I'd been surprised to see him with them when they came into the Blue Bear. Wee Willie was up to something.

I heard a whack and turned back to the fight. Gainey had landed a punch to Sam's gut, and I could see Sam sucking air as he backpedaled. Gainey closed and Sam tied him up, and they went round and round, Gainey's big legs pushing Sam wherever he wanted, but Sam had his shoulder up in Gainey's face, rubbing the rough cloth over his cut lip and butting up with it into Gainey's nose. Gainey was grunting like a bear now, whoofing and chuffing as he tried to whip free of Sam's arms and level him with a clean swing. He threw a knee at Sam but Sam had his hip cocked and blocked it, then let loose of Gainey and spun away to the right again, and as Gainey came for him, he planted himself and threw a left–right combination, the left skinning off Gainey's cheek-bone but the right coming across solid on the side of Gainey's jaw, whap, and Gainey's head snapped and his eyes went gaga for an instant.

It was as solid a shot as I've seen, smack on the button, but Gainey didn't go down. He shook his head and gulped, and his eyes came back to focus.

His face was a mess, though. Both eyes were swollen now, and his eyebrow split bone-deep as well as his lip. His right ear was big as an artichoke and there was blood all down his skivvy shirt and on the dock in weird ropy splatters, like someone had spilled a can of Thirty Weight. He stood there breathing hard, and you could almost hear his mind ticking.

"Had enough, Fatstuff?" Sam asked him. His hands were raw and swollen, and I could see his heart thumping against the wet T shirt. He had his Clark Gable grin on now, but I knew he couldn't last. He knew it too.

Just then, Wee Willie burst out of the crowd behind Sam and grabbed him around the elbows, sliding the swab handle in as a crossbar.

"Take him, Cap!"

Gainey moved in, his eyes glinting through the fat lids, but I got between them and felt his right arm come across taking me on the neck as my own right landed on his ear, and then he and I were tied up, him stinking of sweat and blood and stale salmon, and I brought my knee up into his groin, feeling his balls give against my kneecap, and I swung around as he went over and clubbed him on the back of the neck. I turned and I couldn't see Sam, but Willie was coming at me with the swab handle and I ducked, but it caught me across the side of the face and I saw the lights shatter and fell back on the splintery boards of the dock. I saw Sam belly down, groping in a crab pot over the dock. Then Gainey was on me, retching and gouging, pounding me in the side, and I got my thumbs into his eyeballs and pushed until he backed off, seeing Willie's feet dancing around and feeling the stick whacking on my shoulders and head. I heard a gun go off close by—Norman, I thought, firing to break up the melee. The crowd was all around us now, hands grabbing and pulling and people screaming and cursing, fists splatting on faces, and I broke loose of Gainey, skidding on my palms through a pool of blood and puke and something that felt mushy with sharp bits of rock in it, and Gainey's weight was off me. My hand touched metal and I grabbed it and stood up.

"Christ! You plugged him!" Norman grabbed me, his hand like a claw.

The crowd fell back and I stood there, reeling, and looking at the horror on their faces. Then I looked down. The back of Gainey's head was gone. Just a black gooey hole there, with hair matted around the edges. The pistol was in my hand. Someone stuck out a boot and rolled Gainey over onto his back. There was a blue hole in his cheek, just under his staring right eye, a hole edged with the black of powder burns.

Sam was gone.

LaFourche took the gun from my hand. It was Sam's .357 Colt all right. He flipped the gate and checked the cylinder. One empty brass, smoking.

"I didn't shoot him," I said, but it sounded weak. If I didn't, who did? Sam, of course. But I couldn't say that.

Where the hell was he?

"We'd better go back in the bar," said Norman Ormandy. He wouldn't look me in the face. "I'm going to have to get on the raddio."

I looked at my hands. They were slippery with blood and

brains, Gainey's brains, where I'd skidded through them on the dock. Red-handed, I thought. So that's what it means.

Five minutes later, the shakes set in.

Ten minutes, while drinking a beer in Norman's kitchen, and I began to feel the sting of the powder burns on my wrist and forehead.

A minute later, we heard the drone of the Dakota's engines, boring overhead and then banking east, toward Canada.

CHAPTER ELEVEN

*I*T TOOK the better part of three weeks for that pussel-gutted numbskull Earl Ledbetter, the federal marshal, fetid in his chalk-stripe rumpsprung double-breasted suit and the tie ragged at the knot with a quid of Red Man in his sallow cheeks and tobacco stains on his cracked patent leather oxfords and his vacuous yellow-veined pale blue eyes that never looked at anything with a comprehending glance but rather pored and puzzled over the simplest sight, to conclude what any fool could plainly see: I hadn't dropped the hammer on Gainey Olds. Even at that, he worded his report on the shooting so ambiguously that the CAA had no choice but to lift my commercial pilot's license. Hardly a tragedy as far as I was concerned. We'd become little more than airborne truck drivers, Healey and I, and the air freight business was so hectic now with the Arctic DEW Line bases going in and new mining companies and canneries opening everywhere in the state that I'd had no time to spend back in the bush, which was where I wanted to be. They issued a bench warrant for Healey's arrest for manslaughter and let me go. I still had the Cessna, though I owed Hank Maynard for rigging the floats.

"Uh, how'd you like to go out and watch the bears?"

"At the dump?"

"No. I had the Alugiak in mind."

To my amazement, she agreed.

Josey Poole. Twenty-six. Schoolteacher from Pismo Beach, California. Navy brat. Her father, a career gunner's mate, had gone down with the *Juneau* off Savo Island in the Solomons, the same night action when the Japs came down the Slot and killed the famous Sullivan brothers in the same ship. But not before he'd taught her how to shoot and fish and get around on her own.

Because it was necessary now to get into the bush, she knew it, away from the sleaze and torn toilet paper of the coastal settlements, just California moving north, fags running saloons, fat cops wheezing and spitting in the year-round mud, chalk-stripes and D-7 Cats and the stink of the cannery like someone had peed on the sky, brown bears mangy and ropy with dirty yellow Shirley Temple curls poking through the garbage, and the forever of the fog off the Gulf with the distant bitching cries of the sea lions aching in her ears, yes away into the bush up to the ice: at least there it would be clean and cold.

"I owe Maynard for the floats."

"So?"

"We'll have to kill some bears this fall, pay him off."

"Jim dandy."

At sixty bucks a hide, we'd have to kill ten of them. The first was a glossy black bear, smacking salmon out of a riffle on a clear bright afternoon, leaning at the edge of the run with his muscles rippling under the sheen of the fur, cinnamon snout almost red in the clarity of the day, and she took him clean just in front of the ear with a fifty-yard shot from the Johnson so that he simply slumped forward as if in a doze, his jaws lolling and then a trickle of saliva looping down into the rushing blue water.

"I'll do him."

She worked the knife in around his asshole, leaning over him naked to the waist, her tits lolling pale and a shag of hair under her armpits, nipples stiff with the breeze and the spray of the rapids shining on her pale skin, grunting as she ripped the knife guided by her fingertips up along his shaggy belly, until she had him laid open from tailbone to chin. She grunted again as she peeled the hide back from the pink translucent meat where the rib bones bulged, then ran the knife carefully up the integument until the gray-green coils of gut bulged through, her arms up to the shoulder into his throat to cut the windpipe. Crich.

There's a lot of guts in a bear. She pried the mess loose with strong fingers and together we rolled him on his side so that the innards of him flopped out onto the rock. Christ, how he stank! Then we peeled the hide the rest of the way off of him, skinning out around the nose and ears and the big flabby pink lips that showed his young white strong teeth, and around the eyelids. She was expert.

"That doesn't bother you?"

"Why should it?"

"All the blood. The guts."

"Ah, that's sissy stuff," she said laughing. She shook the long dark hair away from her eyes and knelt there, bloody to the shoulders, the knife easy in her hand, white teeth and those wide green eyes, her little breasts hard and round and paleshadowed down where they met her ribs.

"I killed it and I gutted it and I skinned it and now all we have to do is drag it on out of here and eat it."

"You'd better get that blood off."

"Indeed," she said. "Cleanliness. Godliness."

We were both pretty bloody by then, the bear blood drying fast in the breeze and browning us up like old gilt statues, and she stripped off her slacks, lovely curple, pale, a silken bush on her, then we walked down the rocks to a back eddy and I could feel myself stiffening but it was all so matter of fact that I didn't embarrass myself with a full one, and she plunged in head first, whoofing and barking like a seal, the water eating the dried blood off of her shoulders in yellow flaking rivulets, her hair sleeked back and her teeth shining, and I dove in after her, caught her about the waist with my hands, our feet skidding and slipping on the greasy cold rock of the river's edge, and kissed her, cold lips, hot tongue, and the roar of the rapids and then the sliding brush of a passing, dying salmon.

"Think you could do it treading water?"

"I'll give it a try," I said.

She bellied up to me, her arms light around my neck, wrapping her thighs over my hips as I feathered my hands and kicked dog fashion, upright flutter kick, and found my way into her. It was passing strange, the cold swirling water and then the hot entry, and the two of us spinning slowly in the back eddy, cold lips, hot tongue, gooseflesh and the slow steady deep working hip to hip, the dying salmon circling and eagles overhead, waiting to get hungry enough to eat, the dead eyes of the bear glazed and staring up into the sky, the crash of water bulging over unseen rocks just over her shoulder, her head bent back throat broken yingyang yelping over the roar of the Alugiak as I spent and spawned my love away into her. And then, again, the bear staring, skinned and deadeyed, into the sky.

The gazing eagles.

"How was that?"

"Damn fine."

"Better than the girls in India?"

"I never tried it in the Brahmaputra."

"Or the Ganges?"

"Ganja, yes. Ganges, no."

"But really . . ."

"You don't have to worry."

"But I do, I do. My nose is too long and my teeth are too big and I've got funny motes in my eyes, and sometimes I think I walk funny."

"I never saw it."

"That's because I'm a witch. A bitch of a witch."

"I never saw that either."

"Tell me about the first time you did it. You're not saying much, and I like to hear you talk!"

The fire was dying down now and the bear hide where we had it stretched on a frame of popple poles loomed darker than night against the blue-glowing loom of the glacier. We had dined on cutthroat trout and bear loin, finishing off with a can of Queen Anne cherries that we'd left to chill in the icy water of the river, stiffened and fierce with brandy. We lay naked in front of the fire, under a Four Point blanket and on top of the sleeping bags. The Cessna bobbed at its moorings, tied down to a wind-weathered snag in the gravel shallows just downstream, its floats pucking and whapping on the back riffles of the roaring current.

"Maggie Cruel."

"Not really?"

"Something like that. It was after the prom, on a back road near a gravel quarry just outside of East Periwinkle, Vut. Vut stands for Vermont. When you abbreviate it on an envelope."

"What did she look like?"

"Short, but put together, with reddish hair and a heart-shaped face, nice tits, a bit of a snob. She'd been dating the track star at our high school. But then they got caught in the sack and she was sent away to a private school. He took up with another girl, doctor's daughter, and then one night he was driving home from a date along Route 100 where it winds and bends through the black hills and the old quarries outside of Rochester and he tried to pass an empty semi, but the truck batted him out onto the shoulder and another car was coming, and bingo! Head on. Broke his neck. Finished."

"But the girl."

"Not now. Some other time. It's hard to live in the head on a night like this."

The following morning we set to work building the cabin. We laid it out on a level patch of well-drained ground above the high-water mark of the spring runoff, right at the juncture of the clear river and the glacial river. We gathered ice-ground boulders and, the day being fair, Josey mixed "mud" with the Portland cement I'd brought along in the hold of the Cessna while I laid the corner pilings. The rivers provided an abundance of natural "bank run" aggregate and plenty of good-sized pole timber, much of it already skinned and dried. The heaviest baulks I squared with an adze for the sills, securing the sills to the stone corner pilings with heavy anchor bolts sunk in a wet concrete core.

Josey was a good worker, wiry and indefatigable, never complaining even when I clumsily dropped a heavy boulder on her foot one morning. She had drawn her time at the cannery, quit, and figured to stay up on the river with me for the rest of the summer.

"I can't pay you."

"Don't be a ninny."

We notched the logs for the end walls and side walls, framing in the door and the two south-facing windows with finished lumber I'd bought up from Gurry Bay. For now, the door was the hide of Josey's bear and the windows tacked Plexiglas until we could get real glass from town. When the walls were ten courses high, we roofed them with pole timber and shingled them Tlingit fashion with flattened slabs of spruce bark. In the course of our hunting expeditions in the low hills north of the cabin, we found a stand of yellow cedar. We camped there for a week while I split out rough planks from a well-cured blowdown and Josey killed two more bears, again both blacks. We lived on roast of bear and bear jerky, on Indian rice and Arctic grayling and trout. Our skins burned black with the constant sun, crosshatched with scabbed slashes from devil's club and bug bites, and our clothing at the end of those weeks of hard labor hung on us in fringed tatters, and she loved it.

We floated the planks down a brook to the clear river, and then down to the cabin. I built a door while Josey floored the cabin with the bulk of the planks. We sanded them down with ancient pumice from a long-dormant volcano. Using an empty fifty-five-gallon oil drum for a cistern, we rigged a gravity-feed waterline to the cabin from a spring on the slope behind it, running the water for now through a length of rubber garden hose. Later, I would install galvanized pipe. Another drum, cut in half with a blowtorch, lengthwise, became a sink and a washtub. A third drum evolved, with the addition of a cast-iron door and thimble and a ten-foot length of sheet-metal eight-inch pipe, into a wood stove. It rested on a cradle I'd welded together of scrap iron, over a hearth of river slate. We chinked the walls with gray, slippery glacial mud that dried hard as putty and at night, when the temperature fell, and the chill wind blew down from the glacier, the barrel stove roared and it was warm enough in the low-ceilinged, sixteen-by-twenty-foot cabin to walk around naked in full comfort.

With some more cedar planking, I built a rough table and

a bed frame that we strung with dried bear guts, two big comfortable wooden chairs covered with bear hide, and a deep cupboard where we stowed tools, utensils, ammo and our few books. The days were rapidly growing shorter now, and in the high country back of the glacier the aspens had gone yellow. Big storms moved in over the mountains, and when we woke in the mornings we could see the snow line moving down steadily, a few hundred yards a day. We read at night by the weak yellow light of candles made from bear tallow.

"I'm not going back to California."

"No?"

"I couldn't take it, not after this. All those people. Cars. Movies. Newspapers and radio programs and noise noise noise."

"I was figuring on wintering over up here. I reckon on trapping the valley back of the cedars, maybe a hundred traps. I'll need dogs for that, and a good sled, not to mention the traps and supplies for the winter. I figured on selling the plane and having someone fly me back in with the dogs and gear and then not coming out until breakup or maybe later."

"You don't have to sell the plane. I've got four thousand that Norman's holding for me back in town. Would that be enough?"

"Plenty. But it can be very bad up here in the winter. I've never wintered in the bush, but it's got to be worse than Vermont. Back home, people used to scrag themselves right and left during the winter. Women would drink carbolic acid. The old boy would go out to milk the cows and when he didn't come back after a while, she'd go out there and find him dangling from the rafter, with his tongue stuck out. Sometimes they'd shoot each other. They drank a lot and died from that. Radio helped some, and the telephone, but still it was pretty bad unless you could live inside your head and you had a lot of love for the person you were living with, and for the kids. Up here it'll be worse."

"Except we've got us."

"Yes. But we'd better stock up on a lot of new books just to be sure."

"Come on over here."

She was hot and smooth under the blanket, slicked up and waiting.

"We'll make it," she whispered later. "No doubt about it."

"How do you know?" I whispered back.

"Because I'll use my witchly bitchly powers to make you think you have a harem of a thousand women, each one more beautiful and practiced in the arts of love than the last."

"The arts of love make mighty thin soup."

"And when you're out on the trapline, I'll be running right with you and skinning for you and tanning moose hides and cooking big feasts for you and tending your salmon nets in the summer, splitting the salmon and drying them on the racks the way Indians do, mending your clothes, and you'll teach me how to fly the plane so that I can fly into town if we need anything like more ammo or books or things for around the house. That sort of thing."

"Why don't we get married?"

"Naw," she said. "I'm not ready for that yet."

Her fingers toyed with the bearclaw necklace on my chest. Charlie Blue was right. It had taken me where I wanted to go and made everything all right.

CHAPTER TWELVE

IN MID-OCTOBER, the snow began to fly. Anchor ice formed on the river edges and floes thickened in the mainstream. The last geese blew with the last of the aspen leaves, skeining south through iron skies, their distant yap skirling down through snow-thick winds. We had not yet laid in our meat for the winter and took advantage of the snow to drift the river in the nineteen-foot aluminum freight canoe we'd picked up on our shopping spree in Anchorage. We ghosted with the ice floes, Josey hunched in the bow with the new .30/06 full-stocked Mannlicher carbine across her knees while I steered in the stern and fended off the ice as best I could to keep it from clanking on the hull. Dead silence except for the gurgle of black water around roots and rocks; the shorelines dark gray broken-toothed ranks of spruce shifting and fading and then emerging clear through the veils of snow; a raven calling somewhere in the gloom.

The moose, when he finally appeared, stood hock-deep in the water with sedge drooling from his long bulbed nose, and at first he seemed just another uprooted snag along the shore.

But a faint glint of warmth from the polished spoons of his antlers gave him away. He popped clear to view, as if some shaman had placed him there, had transformed the snag into nearly a ton of hot meat and heavy hide and bone.

Flame crack from the muzzle: a fiery tiger lily, bloomed and blown on the instant: the swat like a well-hit baseball as the 220-grain hollow point bullet took him on the shoulder and he lurched awkwardly, drunk with death, up the bank, water splashing black from his belly and his haunches bulging in the steely light: then a second shot: thump, into the brisket, and he teetered near the edge of the spruce for a moment, shuddered, sprawled forward on his chest with a crash like a falling tree.

"Let it snow," said Josey as we stood in the sweet steam that rose from his open chest cavity, his heart huge and bloody in her hands. "We won't starve now."

And so, like the bears, we settled into our winter den. The sturdy log cache we'd built well away from the main cabin was full to the rafters with frozen slabs of moose and bear, ptarmigan and trout and grayling; cases of canned vegetables and soup lined one wall of the main cabin itself, serving as insulation additional to the rockwool with which we'd lined the ceiling. With her new Singer, Josey had fashioned heavy, bright-patterned shades for the two cabin windows, which were now double-glazed with proper glass. She had bought some house plants—a wandering jew, a piggyback begonia, a spider plant and a velvet plant with its smooth furry purple leaves, an aloe vera whose slimy sap worked wonders on stove-burned fingers; little pots of herbs dangled on hooks from the rafter near the kitchen window, chive, parsley, tarragon, mint, rosemary, thyme, pineapple sage and burnet, all thriving in various combinations of heat and light and cool shadow.

Three walls of the house, outside, were stacked roof-high with ranks of wind-cured firewood, spruce and popple mainly, wood that my childhood neighbors in Vermont would have sneered at as "junk stuff" fit only to sugar with in the springtime. But we had no rock maple, red oak, beech or ash, and I knew if we burned the wood hot enough and kept a close watch on the chimney pipe, cleaning it once a week perhaps, we would avoid the danger of creosote buildup and a chimney fire. A small and niggling point, you may think, but in that country, in the dead of winter with the thermometer bottomed out at seventy below, a fire would be the finish of us, even if we got out alive. Of course, we could make do in the cache, which was one reason we had built it well away from the cabin, but that would be roughing it. As it was, we would winter in luxury.

With rollers and a block and tackle, we had winched the Cessna up a log ramp onto the high ground, and replaced the floats with skis. When the river froze solid, we could fly out again if we had to, but we both agreed we would like to spend the first winter entirely on our own. It would be an adventure of the mind.

We had looted the bookstores of Anchorage. The complete works of Dickens. The Waverley Novels. Shakespeare in a single volume. As much Faulkner as we could find, but most importantly *The Bear.* Agatha Christie and Dorothy B. Sayers. Nordhoff and Hall. Thoreau. Benchley. Turgenev and Tolstoi and Gogol's *Lost Souls. Anguish in Swaziland* by Hubert Beard-Highwood, along with his sister Lavinia's surreal companion volume, *By Lallygag Through Northumberland. Fix Bayonets!* by John W. Thomason, which I mistakenly took for a knife-repair book but enjoyed anyway. *Gray's Anatomy. Blackstone on Law.* A delightful account of early travels in the Arctic titled *Chiaroscuro Motley* by Vassily Sergeevich Volkov, translated from the Russian by Constance Garnett. Louise Helen Tyor's best-selling new cookbook *The Eclectic Kitchen* (the last copy on the shelves in Anchorage, and perhaps all Alaska), into which, we discovered only when we got home, some mischievous printer had bound a totally irrelevant folio of ink sketches portraying the lovely chefette in various stages of deshabille, gaily waving a wooden spoon, clad finally in naught but a garter belt and black mesh stockings, with a white chef's toque cocked jauntily on her pretty, Joseyesque head. It gave us many a laugh over dinner in the months that followed.

The books and the laughter were very important, for the long winter night of the North Country sends electric ghosts and grim-fisted demons leaping over the synapses of the soul. In the depth of winter, the goneaway sun barely edges over

78

the horizon at eleven in the morning, a worn shaved obol from some distant past, and creaks down again without a wink by three in the afternoon. The air lies heavy and still, filling the universe with a creaking cold that fingers the very bowels and crystallizes them; the chimney smoke rises no more than a dozen feet from the pipe, a still, thick blue column, then collapses within itself. You can hear it fall. And you can hear, through the cabin walls, if you are alone in your soul, mourning the dead world, the passing hiss and crackle of the Aurora, whispers in some cobwebbed corner of your mind, insinuations and sly hints of murder and madness: perhaps in all the universe there is only one mind, and it is insane, and to keep itself from exploding like a tree in the taiga that bursts into a million million toothpicks as it freezes, that mad mind had imagined a world. And this mind is you.

"Don't tell me things like that." Josey shivered beside me under the goosedown quilt. The fire snapped in the drum stove and under the cabin the dogs shifted, growled, and nestled back down within the universe of their long silver tails; the spines of our books glowed in the amber umbra of kerosene light; water hissed in the teapot. "Isn't that what Mark Twain believed toward the end of his life, after his daughter died?"

"Something like that. And he had all of Hartford to keep him company."

But we had our work. The trapline mainly: some thirty miles of it, extending in two long, flattened loops that formed a wobbly figure-eight straddling the drainage of Carcajou Creek, our name for the clear stream that flowed into the Alugiak from the northeast. Over that distance, we set 120 traps in the most likely spots we could find—hollow logs near creeks for mink, ledge country for foxes, squirrel den territory for both the ground squirrels that were prized as parka material and for the wolves and lynxes that preyed on them. Our traps were mainly single and double springs, ranging in size from ones and one and a halfs (for weasel and mink) to fours and fives (for lynx and wolf). We boiled them three or four times to remove the human-machined odor of oil and steel, the final boil in a stew of pine and spruce needles. Then we dipped the still-hot traps in melted beeswax and, when it was dry, handled them only in smoked leather gloves that never came indoors. Most of our sets were in cubbies—little hidey-holes we built of spruce boughs, with a bait swinging enticingly at the back of the cubby: a ptarmigan wing, a hunk of spoiled fish, the foot of a beaver. A dangling corncob smeared with peanut butter and honey had worked wonderfully on the raccoons I trapped as a kid in Vermont, but there are no raccoons in Alaska and nobody else up here seemed interested. For them, it was meat or nothing.

We ran the line two or three times a week, depending on weather, covering the double loop in a long, ten-hour day. The dogs—five of them—were Husky crosses, silent, fierce-eyed and quarrelsome, with a lot of wolf in the mix. There was no love lost among us. In the first weeks they fought among themselves, tangling the traces and slowing the run, but we learned to get their attention with stout clubs and harsh voices (Josie cussing like a Marine sergeant) and the more they worked, the more they worked together so that by the time the rivers were frozen solid, we could spot a fight brewing before it began and quell it with a yell. Most of the furbearers we took in our sets were frozen by the time we got to them. Those that weren't, we stunned with a club blow over the bridge of the nose and then finished off by standing on the animal's chest. Wolves and lynxes, growling and hissing at the end of their trap chains, received a quick .22-caliber bullet behind the ear as surcease.

Returning from the run in the dark late one afternoon, the stars crackling overhead and the frost on our wolf-fur parka ruffs stiff and spiky from the exertion, we found a strange sled parked near the cabin, and strange dogs chained back in the trees. A short, busy figure moved against the yellow light behind the windows. We had a visitor. We shucked our snowshoes and went in.

"So you stayed!" yelled Charlie Blue as we came into the cabin. "Good for you! Good for the bearclaw necklace!" He was clad all in fur, his face a vast brown interlocking wrinkle. In one hand, he held a half-cooked haunch of beaver he'd fried over the new woodburning stove and the fat glistened on his jutting chin. I wondered what was left in the larder. Josey looked at me doubtfully, but I gave her a wink.

"I hope you've helped yourself to food and fire," I said to him.

"Naturally, of course, *certainement*. Listen, you're trapping in this country. How are you doing on cross-fox?"

"Not so good."

"Here, try some of this." He pulled a bottle from one of his many pockets and unscrewed the cap. An odor so pungent, so rotten, filled the cabin that one might have expected all the dead of all the world, past present and future, animal vegetable and alien, to have putresced in that tiny phial. "Take salmon eggs, duck livers, seal blubber, some herring and some codfish, deer meat and a few shrew mice. Stick 'em in a jar and let 'em rot together for two years in a warmish place. To get the shrew mice, bait a perforated tin can but don't let 'em get at the bait. They'll die right quick. Won't nip your knuckles when you come to take 'em. Makes a nice oily scent for the fox. Here, you try it. How you doing on wolf?"

"Fair."

"Should be doing better. Too damn many wolf this country. Not enough moose. Wolf eating them all. Here's what you do." He reached into another pocket and pulled out a long rib bone, probably from a moose or maybe a caribou. The top third of the bone was sharpened to a knife edge. "Coat the sharp end in tallow—some good rich bear or beaver fat is best. Stick the bone sharp end up in the snow out where the wolves have been running. Wolf comes up, can't resist licking the fat. Licks down to the sharp part. Slits his tongue. Can't feel it in the cold. Goes off and bleeds to death. You follow out along his track, look for bloody shit. At the end, you'll find dead wolf. No bullet holes in the hide. Get you more mazuma that way."

"What's to keep the wolf from pulling the bone out of the snow and making off with it?"

"Cut a hole through the river ice and hold the blunt end in the water. It freezes in a minute or two and the wolf can't pull it out."

"I hope you'll stay for dinner with us and spend the night," Josey said.

"Of course, *natürlich*. First, I'll feed my dogs. I'll feed your dogs too. Where do you keep your fish?"

"In the cache."

"I looked in there. All your salmon is gone. Everything else is okay, hunky-dory. Some thief must get in while you're gone, steal your salmon. But I've got plenty on my sled. Don't worry." He went out into the night.

"What's going on?" Josey asked. "Did he steal our fish?"

"Not really," I said. I told her about my earlier run-in with him down the river. "Whatever he takes, he'll leave more in return. And better. The necklace brought me you, didn't it?"

The door slammed open and Charlie stumped in, grinning and swatting his furclad arms against his sides.

"Good. They're eating. Plenty of fish for all. You got anymore of that good brandy?"

CHAPTER THIRTEEN

CHARLIE SPENT the night curled in front of the barrel stove, naked except for his bearclaw necklace—the twin of mine—and his mukluks. He was wrinkled all over, like one of those Chinese fighting dogs you see now and then in the photo magazines, all drooped and folded skin so that when another dog grabs one in a fight, it can't get hold of anything vital. He snored in a great rolling cacophony of roars, grunts, gurgles and wheezes, sometimes sounding like a ravening wolf, sometimes like a giant raven. Even our dogs, who usually spent the night growling and snapping at one another, fell silent in awe. At first we could not sleep, but then his snoring took on a kind of rhythm, as if one were dozing at the edge of a great waterfall, or high on a beach where a storm was playing itself out among the rocks below.

We awoke to the smell of frying bear bacon and bubbling oatmeal. Charlie stood at the stove, singing at the top of his voice in what I took to be Tlingit.

"Up! Up!" he yelled on seeing us stir. "Daylight in the

swamp! Let's eat and then I take you into the glacier, show you your own forever cache of dog meat."

He was as good as his word. After we'd eaten, he led us up over the frozen scree slope to the blue face of the glacier itself, and on into a deep crevasse. It was dark and dank in there, slippery going.

"Here," said Charlie. "Here is the entrance." He smiled and ducked his head and crawled inside the twisting vertical ice-edged slot that gaped between the boulders. We followed.

The dark dissipated quickly into a pervasive blue light, day permeating the height of glacier above us, filtered as through a thick lens carved from pure corundum. Muck and ice water soaked our knees, but soon the twisting passage angled upward, and we clawed our way along, using elbows and toes and the waning friction of wet mukluks until we began to skid more than we climbed.

"Grab this," said Charlie. I groped and felt a curved projection, cold as the ice but grooved to accept the clutch of my fingers. I heaved myself up on it and reached back for Josey. Above us through the blue shadows, I could see an irregular ladder of these semicircular protuberances, some closer together, others a short leap apart. Then it came to me: this was ivory.

Above us, hundreds of feet of ice above us, the sun broke through the cloud and the intensity of the light in the tunnel went up by megalumens. Through the ice wall, I saw dim shapes from which the ivory circles grew, slope-backed, thick-legged, elephantine, hairy. We were climbing a ladder of mammoth tusks. A smell of rotting meat wafted down the tunnel from the exposed flanks of animals long buried, creatures wandering on crusted earth-covered ice in the thawing of that time, who crashed through into the crevasses, caught these many millennia in the deepfreeze of my glacier.

"Chaw a hunk," said Charlie, grinning. He had whittled a sliver of mammoth meat from the exposed flank, close to the ice where it was still fresh. I took it and chewed. The meat was rich and red and, as it thawed in my mouth, it tasted sweet. It could have used some salt and pepper. Josey tried some and agreed.

"We'll have to bring some back to the cabin," she whispered as Charlie climbed ahead. "Mammoth tartare!"

Farther up, my eyes growing accustomed now to the fact of frozen prehistory within the ice, I discerned the shape of a huge, bobtailed cat, broke-legged on its back, its foot-long fangs angling out so that one of them stuck through the ice and served as a convenient handhold. Above it, barely visible, the figure of a giant dog—a dire wolf, no doubt victim of the thaw.

Cave bears, giant sloths, long-horned bison, marmots the size of calves; here a great beaver grinning bucktoothed out of the wall, its ears rotted, its eyes like floating opals; there a small and ugly horse no bigger than a Labrador retriever with a square, unfinished head and the stripes of a quagga.

Our voices, as we murmured awestruck in this miraculous gloom, echoed down the twisting tunnel, rose back to our ears as faroff hisses, so that it was easy to imagine the dead creatures themselves muttering and sighing in their icy jail, denied the freedom of entropy.

We emerged finally into a cavern. The light was much brighter now and half-thawed bones littered the floor. The sour smell of cold rot pervaded the room, such as one whiffs on opening a long-uncleaned freezer. The legs, tails and flanks of animals showed through the ice, in some places masked by only a shallow film of it, in others protruding through into the open air.

"Plenty meat here," Charlie said. "Good meat too. These animals no longer live on the earth, but they are not poison. Many times I feed them to my dogs, eat the meat myself. It's good! Rich meat! Good as whale meat!"

His voice echoed and reechoed through the cavern and down the long tunnel we had followed. The ice creaked and groaned in response. Josey squeezed my hand and I too was fearful that Charlie's decibels would bring the whole glacier tumbling down around our ears. The few times we had shot a rifle near the ice, we had sent small seracs snapping and tumbling down the glacier's snout.

"But this meat you better not eat," he said, his voice falling to a whisper. He led us over to the far corner of the cavern and pointed up into the gloom. Staring down at us through the blue ice was a human face. It was that of a white man, heavily mustachioed, his eyes not much darker than the ice that locked him in his grave. On his head was a sombrero with a chin strap stretched taut by his gaping jaw, his mouth wide open as if he were still yelling with the fall down the crevasse that had killed him. His broken limbs were clad in what appeared to be a heavy chain-stitched wool sweater, corduroy trousers stagged into cleated leather boots, and around his neck a set of smoked glasses of the sort Arctic explorers use to prevent snowblindness. One hand had melted free of the ice at some previous time and it groped out into the air above us, fleshless, but with a few cold-withered tendons still clinging to the clawlike bones.

"That's Doctor Moran," whispered Charlie. "A great shaman in his own country, but worse than a fool up here."

"Did you know him?" Josey asked.

"Like a brother," Charlie answered. "A stubborn, younger brother who will not listen. This was in the days of the Stampede, '98 or '99, and I was down on the coast then. I was very poor, trying to live like a white man. Doctor Moran had bought a map that showed lost gold fields in the mountains behind the glacier. He asked me to guide him and his men over the ice. The men he had picked himself after much searching in New York, where he came from. One man knew all about rocks. Another how to build tools of steel. A third could bend tin into useful shapes. They all knew how to read. They all were very big and very weak, though Doctor Moran said they had worked hard at exercise before leaving their homes. I didn't know what exercise was. To me, it meant living. They were stupid as well as weak. I told Doctor Moran that there was no gold over the glacier. 'How do you know?' he asked. 'Would I be here in Gurry Bay, poor and listening to nonsense, if there were?' I answered.

"But I agreed to take them over the ice. For dogs they had six large, weak ones from New York. Saint Bernards and Newfoundlands, I learned they were called. They were bigger than wolves but weak as wolf puppies when their eyes are still closed and they wiggle and whine in the den smelling of sour milk and spittle. Each of the men had a thousand pounds of food and equipment. They also had a great huge motor-driven sled that was so heavy that they left it on the beach. Such fools have rarely come to this country, though recently we have been seeing more of them.

"We came up the river to the glacier. They pulled everything up on top. Days passed, weeks passed. Then it was all up there and they found the dogs could scarcely move the sledges. Blizzards blew in off the sea. They waited them out. The sun broke through and the men began to turn red, their skin peeling away in long slippery tatters. Some went snowblind. More storms. The men began to go mad. They found one strangled out on the ice. His partner said a 'glacier monster' had appeared out of the driving snow and attacked them.

"Weeks passed, then months. Soon it was winter again and still they were on the glacier. Men walked out into the storms to die. You will find them somewhere here in the ice. When their food was nearly gone—though there was plenty of food just a day's march on snowshoes off the glacier, down in the protected valleys, as you two have seen—they decided to make a final dash across the ice to the valley of the lost gold. I told them there was no gold. They called me a fool and a liar.

" 'If you go ahead in weather like this, you will fall into the mouths of the ice bear,' I told them. They went ahead. I went back. You see what became of them."

He sighed and reached up to touch the bony fingers.

"The only 'glacier monster' was in their bellies. The hunger for gold."

We set to work cutting slabs of mammoth meat from the protruding flesh and skidded a good-sized pile of it back down the passageway. Charlie helped us carry it to the cache and stow it. There was enough now to tide us through the rest of the winter, dogs and humans alike.

"That ivory is valuable," I told Charlie as he harnessed his dogs and prepared to leave downriver.

"*Vraiment, certes!*" he bellowed. "Do you need money? Do you need a thousand professors from a thousand museums from all over creation pouring in here to examine those carcasses? Try that fox scent I gave you. It is quieter."

He whipped up his lean, wolf-eyed team and slithered out onto the frozen Alugiak, the Aurora arching and surging above him as he sang and roared his way into the nearly-always night.

The next day, while Josey went out on snowshoes to hunt willow ptarmigan along the Alugiak, I stayed behind to mend a binding on the sled runner. When I was finished, I went back up into the cavern. The day was bright and the light much more intense than on our earlier visit, and I counted fully two dozen mammoths buried in the ice, ranging in size from an infant as big as a Buick to great tuskers with ivory that possibly weighed two hundred pounds the side. The herd must have crashed through the ice in panic, pursued perhaps by a pack of dire wolves. In the big cave, I avoided Doctor Moran's eyes and picked up the tip of a tusk that had cracked off and fallen to the floor. It was smooth and heavy, the color of old gold; a shard of the dead past in that eerie underwater light: palpable antiquity.

CHAPTER FOURTEEN

THUS BEGAN what I have come to call, after the manner of certain painters, my "Greed Period." It was fortunately brief, but its intensity and the agony with which it ended made the scars sting all the more smartly. I could not get that ivory out of my mind.

Josey was all she had promised to be, a harem and a half of sensual variety and delight. At a time when most women doled out their favors with a sour parsimony (we could have called it "scrooging" in those days), demanding payment in the coin of guilt and gratitude, she gave and gave and gave until I hurt. Not that I'm complaining: it was a delicious exhaustion, a fine frazzling, and we were so full of pep—charged with the cold electricity that comes from a hundred miles a week at a dog trot on snowshoes, chuffing in clouds of crackling steam, wreathed in the smoke and snowspume thrown back by our racing dogs, reading and decrypting at a run the hieroglyphs of other hardy animals traveling the snows—that when we returned to the warmth of the cabin, spicy with its smell of herbs and of the moose stew bubbling on the stove, our hunger for one another was indistinguishable from that we felt for our food. And often the moose stew was only dessert.

So I should have been content. We were happy and in love. The cabin was snug and we had plans for many improvements. Thanks to Charlie's fox lure, the trapline was producing enough furs to keep us in store-bought supplies for the coming year. (I couldn't bring myself to use his wolf-killing technique; the very thought of it made my tongue pucker.) Nonetheless, as the winter wore along, I grew itchy.

Some of it, I knew, was that Healey's disappearance with the Dakota had left me on my own for the first time in my life. From the farm, I had gone to an even more rigid life, the air corps, and from there to the mindless back and forth of air transport, with Sam making most of the major decisions. Now, I was feeling the need to prove myself, to show myself and the world that I could succeed on my own without Sam's help.

The enthusiasm I had felt that first night as Sam and I camped below the glacier discussing our hunting and fishing lodge came back full force. American sportsmen had been frustrated for the better part of fifteen years, first by the Depression and then by World War II, both of which kept them hunting and fishing pretty much in their own backyards. Or on the battlefield for enemies. Now, with the wave of affluence and high hopes that followed the war, they were out and around, spending money they had never dreamed of earning on safaris and shikars to Africa and India, on big-game hunts and wilderness fly-in fishing trips in Canada and Alaska. Lodges sprang up all over the North Country, from the Labrador, where huge world-record brook trout lurked in crystalline flowages, to the bare, high spine of the Continent, the sheep country of Alberta and British Columbia and Alaska where Bighorn and Dall and Stone sheep clattered their curl-and-a-half horns, where huge moose and towering bears and herds of long-legged, forest-browed caribou wandered, all of them innocent after years of peace while the world of man was at war.

Our country, there under the glacier, was ideal. When the winter settled in for good, with cold, heavy, windless air and clear skies, we rolled out the Cessna, refilled her oil sump, and went up to scout the country from the sky. Josey took to flying as she did to everything else: with high enthusiasm and low-keyed, quick-study competence. In the bare foothills of the Dead Mountie Range not twenty minutes flying time from the cabin, we found clots and clusters of wintering Dall sheep, browsing on the windcleared slopes for lichens and moss, their wool looking like skiffs of snow against the olive rock, the rams' horns catching the low light in rings of frozen honey. Flying down the intervales, we spotted bands of moose yarded up in the dwarf willow and popple, gazing up at us with their huge hammer heads and stupid, bovine eyes. They looked in good shape. The winter, harsh as it seemed to us at times, had been gentle on them.

Except for the wolves. Charlie Blue was right, there were too many of them in the country. I read, nowadays, that wolves are truly a benefice in the wild, that they kill only the weak, the old and the sick, thus working nature's cruel pruning shears on a moose herd to strengthen it. Somehow, it didn't look that way to us. We saw wolf bands harrying big, strong moose that were neither sick nor old nor weak enough to keep from running miles through deep snow, the moose turning at last to fight off the circling, slashing wolves for an hour more before falling finally to a severed tendon and the gut-seeking jaws of the hunters.

"Let's take a couple of those bastards," I said one afternoon to Josey. We were flying at low level over a long, wide valley between two steep ridges. Below us, four wolves loped after a lone moose that sank nearly belly deep in the snow with every lunge. The wolves were padding easily on the surface crust, biding their time until the moose would be too winded to run anymore and would have to turn and fight. I landed on the skis well behind the chase and removed the door while Josey checked the Mannlicher. Then we took off again and caught up with the wolves.

"I'll take her back to nearly stall speed when we come up on them," I yelled to her over the roar of the wind. "Pop the lead wolf first and see what the others do." She nodded and leaned out the door, held by her seat belt but with her head out in the slipstream, the rifle at her shoulder and her elbows braced on her knees, and as we eased past the running wolves that looked up out of the corners of their eyes, their tongues lolling and tails flat out behind them, she shot—snow spurted ahead of the lead wolf and he kept going—and then worked the bolt, the brass flying back into the cockpit, and corrected her aim, shot again and rolled the wolf sideways in the snow, him biting at his shoulder where the bullet had smashed him, then lying doggo, or dead. The other wolves kept running.

"Take the next one."

I circled and came back in behind them again.

Pow! Another one down.

The two remaining wolves slowed, looking up and around, then angled off toward the ridge to their right. We let them go, circling back and landing to skin out the two Josey had shot. Two more hides for the wolf bale, plus fifty dollars apiece in federal bounty, and one moose spared to breed again.

But furs alone would not bring in enough money to expand the cabin into the lodge I had in mind, nor would they pay for the boats and motors and generator and freezer and pack-horses and all the other things necessary to turn Carcajou Creek into a successful hunting and fishing lodge. So my mind kept circling back to that ivory.

Josey was against it.

"You know Charlie's right," she said. "The moment you try to sell one of those tusks, a thousand paleontologists will learn about it. They'll be in here like black flies, with government backing, and they'll either kick us out of here or at best buy us out."

"Maybe there's a black market. Norman Ormandy knows a guy in Anchorage who smuggles deer and caribou antlers out of the country, sells them to Red China and Taiwan. The Chinese make soup out of them. They believe that it gives them vigor, better hard-ons, something like that. Especially when the antlers are still in velvet."

"I thought one of the main reasons you came north was to get away from that kind of crap." She was angry now, her eyes sparking. "You get tied up with the black market and you're no better than those sleazy operators on the Outside that you're always bitching about."

"It would only be until we got the lodge built the way we want it."

"It's hackneyed to say it, I know, but you can't build a palace on a swamp. Ends and means. Like that. And you haven't asked me how I feel about the hunting lodge to begin with. How do you know I want to hang around the lodge all day washing dishes and changing sheets and cooking three-star dinners for some fat cats from Dallas or Baton Rouge while you lead them around by the hand to plug moose and bears?" She was up and pacing now, high color in her cheeks, and I knew she wanted to slug me. I'll bet she could hit a ton.

"Honey," I said, trying to laugh. "We're having our first fight."

"Fucking A," she said, turning and squaring at me, her hands on her hips. "And don't tell me I'm beautiful when I'm mad or I'll paste you one in the chops."

The daughter of a gunner's mate, sure as shooting.

"You don't pronounce the terminal *g* in that," I said.

"In what?" She started and blinked.

"Fuckin' A," I said.

Then we both laughed and I hugged her, and I told her that if she was against it I wouldn't do it.

But still the idea was there, and growing.

The days grew longer now and the chinooks began to blow in from the sea, warm wet winds that turned the snow from fine grit that squeaked like mice underfoot to heavy, web-clogging sludge. The rivers rose under the ice and we could not run the sled on them for fear of overflows—layers of water forced up over the ice and unfrozen in long stretches. If you ran into one of them, you soaked your mukluks up to the knees. It was still cold enough at night so the overflow water froze to a thin skin on top. Wet feet were doom in that country all the way up to mid-April. So the trapping season was over, and breakup not far off when we decided to fly into Gurry Bay for a resupply run and to sell our furs. Norman Ormandy had promised me as good a price as I could hope to get in Anchorage or Sitka or Ketchikan.

"Twelve fifty," said Norman Ormandy, sucking the end of a pencil. "For the lot."

"Twelve fifty? Last summer we were talking two, three grand."

"Don't blame me," he chirped, shooting his eyebrows. "I don't decide the fashions. What they want down there is ranch mink, chinchilla, Persian lamb and silver fox. Wolf is out. Lynx is out. You couldn't sell a full-blanket beaver for a doormat. I can't help it what they wear Outside."

"Give me another slug of rum," I told him.

We were sitting at the bar in the Blue Bear, Norman and Josey and I plus four hefty bales of worthless fur. It was raining along the coast and I was worried that breakup might come sooner than we'd figured. Already there was just snow enough left on the airstrip to land safely with skis. Now this with the furs.

Josey was reading a letter that had arrived for her over the winter from Outside. She hadn't paid much attention to what we were saying.

"What if I were to take them up to Anchorage?"

"I'm giving you Anchorage prices, Jack," Norman said. "If you were some Indian or Eskimo, I'd give you a grand, tops. Believe."

I had to believe him. Norman knew that if I found out he'd japped me on the furs, I'd be back in no time to ream him a new asshole. The one he had suited him just fine.

"That'll barely pay my supplies for next year," I said.

"Things are tough all over," Norman answered. "It's the Cold War. The only real market we had for a lot of these furs was Eastern Europe, and now they passed a law we can't trade with them anymore. In Europe, all the ladies are wearing leopard. You see any leopards up there last winter?"

"Don't get cute."

Josey folded her letter and slid it back into the envelope. She looked pale.

"I've got to go over to the Western Union," she said, sliding down from the stool.

"What's up?"

"I'll tell you later." She walked out of the Blue Bear, stiff and proper, a town girl once again.

"Listen, Norman. You remember you were telling me once about that guy up in Anchorage who sold stuff to the Chinese? Antlers and stuff?"

"Yeah. Mister Fong. He does a good business. Why? You got some horn?"

"Maybe," I said. "What does he pay?"

"Good money. Eight or ten bucks a pound if it's in full velvet. He pays a good buck for walrus ivory too, but he doesn't see that much of it anymore. The herd is down to only about fifty thousand and most of the Eskimos are working in the canneries or on construction nowadays. But you got no walruses up on the glacier—and I'm not being cute."

"Where does he hang out, this Fong?"

"He's got a warehouse down on the docks by the Inlet," Norman said. "He's in the phone book. You want another?"

He poured me another rum and popped a beer for me. "On the house," he said. I must have looked pretty mean, coming in there after a winter in the bush, my beard full and bristly now and my face brown and seamed from windburn and snowglare.

"You hear anything about Healey?" I asked him.

"Someone said he was down in Juneau a while back. I hear he's got some biggies working to get the charge dropped."

"What happened to Marie?"

"She hung around here a while getting sloshed until her money was gone. I paid her fare up to Anchorge to get some new teeth. She never came back."

"Probably peddling her hips up in the Big Town."

"Something like that."

We sat there for a bit, me drinking and Norman polishing glasses, and then Josey came back in. She stood inside the door and I went over to her.

"My mother's very sick," she said. Her voice was tight and she was holding herself together. "I've got to fly down to San Francisco."

"Hell," I said. What do you say?

"I'm sorry, Jack, really, but I've got to go down there. I don't think she'll last long. That letter was from my sister. She's practically nuts, taking care of her, and . . ."

"What?"

"They need money." She nearly choked on that, and looked down at the floor. I put my arm around her.

"Take the fur money."

"No. I couldn't do that. There's some money left from last summer, a thousand or so. That should help them some."

"You'll take the fur money."

CHAPTER FIFTEEN

THOUGH MISTER Fong was very old—he told me he had come to Alaska as a young man to work on the old White Pass & Yukon Railroad back in '98—he seemed no more than middle-aged. His thick hair was dyed a gaudy purplish black that caught the glint of the kerosene lamps lighting his godown on the wharves of Cook Inlet. His face was seamless and his tiny black eyes gleamed bright as a muskrat's. Ancient bronze bowls crisscrossed with fine engraving adorned his desk and a jade horse the size of a small terrier stood on the mantle over a glowing coal fire. He poured me a glass of wine from a tall slim bottle.

"Snake wine," he said. "A sure cure for dandruff and falling hair, but delicious in its own right." Sure enough, there were small snakes coiled and pickled in the bottom of the bottle. The rice wine had a musky, mildewed taste to it like very old champagne that's lost its sizzle, but it went down smoothly and it certainly set the scalp atingle. If Healey were still around, I'd have offered to buy a couple of bottles. He loved anything Chinese. "Now about that ivory, Mister . . ."

"Johnson," I said. "Sam Johnson." If the deal went through, I didn't want him tracking me down through the homestead records. "I was hunting sheep up in the Wrangells last fall and I found this chunk of ivory in the rubble of a recent avalanche." I took the fragmented tusk tip from my pocket and placed it on the mahogany desk. "I dug deeper into the rock and found the rest of the tusk and what looked to be the tip of another, but night was coming on and I didn't have time to dig them out. People down the coast told me that you knew something about the worth of ivory."

He picked up the shard and turned it against the light.

"How big was the tusk this came from and how was it shaped?"

"I could see about four, maybe five foot of it, and it was deeply curved, kind of kinked inward toward the tip."

Mister Fong shouted something in Chinese and I heard scurrying back in the godown. In a few moments, the door opened and a young woman in silk robes scuttled into the office, bowing and scraping, and placed a larger piece of ivory in Mister Fong's long-nailed hand. He compared the two. Through the door, I could see a tangle of antlers back in the gloom, tines and beams of caribou and moose and Sitka deer, furry against the yellow light. He dismissed the young woman and sat for a long moment, fingers steepled like stacked spears, his mouth pursed and eyes lidded.

"This is very old ivory, Mister Johnson," he said at last. "Older even than I"—he tittered and nodded—"as you have no doubt guessed. It is the ivory of the woolly mammoth, long extinct, and by rights you should report your find to the territorial government. The tusks would prove invaluable to science. You might even receive a reward." He paused and smiled at me with teeth far whiter than the ivory.

"*You* seem to have kept a piece," I said.

"Yes. A poor Eskimo hunter found it north of the Circle while extending his trapline. Up in the Brooks range, I believe. It found its way to me through the intercession of a minister of the Gospel, serving the heathen in those dreary climes. Men of the cloth are so naive. He never thought to report it to the government."

"How much did you pay him?"

"Fifty dollars." ·

"How much does that work out per pound?"

"Twenty-five."

At two hundred pounds a tusk, that was ten grand a pair. A start, anyway.

"Men of the cloth, as you say, are not of this world," I said. "Perhaps the good padre's needs were fewer than mine. I would expect fifty a pound for the risk of climbing that treacherous scree slope again and removing rocks, any one of which might prove the keystone to another avalanche."

"Far too rich for my old blood, Mister Johnson. In my humble estate, a poor coolie who toiled until his bones were bent on the White Pass & Yukon, who froze with the men on the Chilkoot, who spent all his meager savings over a long lifetime of toil, et cetera, to purchase this miserable, draughty godown, I could afford no more than thirty-five." He poured me another glass of snake wine, smiling brightly, his blood up now with the bargaining. Clearly he loved it, even more than his bronzes and jade and juicy young women.

"That's mean country up there in the Wrangells, Mister Fong. Bears and wolves, winds so cold and fierce they can peel the meat from a man's face, a country that eats airplanes the way you would a bowl of fried noodles. I could not risk the recovery of this ivory for you at any price below forty dollars a pound."

"Thirty-seven fifty and you can take the young lady, my able assistant, with you. Keep her for a couple of weeks, a month even."

"I have a young lady of my own," I said. "Forty or no deal."

He smiled and sighed, the lights mellowing now in his beady eyes like those of a man fading into postcoital languor. "Done." He rose and extended his hand. It felt the way I imagined the hand of Doctor Moran might feel. "Contact me by telephone when you have recovered the goods and we will arrange a suitable rendezvous to complete our transaction." He opened a drawer in the desk and removed a pile of bills, peeled a few off and handed them to me. "Two hundred dollars as a down payment and an earnest of my good faith," he said.

"It was a pleasure doing business with you, Mister Johnson. So few young people seem to enjoy such transactions these days."

When I'd put her on the Northwest Orient Stratocruiser at Merrill Field, southbound from Anchorage to Seattle and points Outside, Josey had promised she'd cable the Blue Bear in a couple of weeks with her return date. I had serious doubts that she would ever come back. Once you get Outside, Alaska begins to fade toward unreality. You tell people what you did up there and they stare at you as if you were speaking in Martian. Eventually, their inability to comprehend induces a kind of amnesia in the uprooted Alaskan, so that he himself begins to doubt his experiences. Whirl and bustle confuse him, comforts pound him into a walking cube steak, he buys a car and a television set, gets a job, a home. Alaska becomes a tale of youthful adventure. Only on cold, frosty nights, alone with the memory of ice and emptiness, does it come alive again, and then only for a single shivering moment.

Fresh snow had fallen when I returned to the cabin on Carcajou Creek. I'd left plenty of meat for the chained dogs, but they cowered at my approach, whining and flinching, avoiding my eyes. Much of their food remained uneaten. I found bear tracks around the cache, and claw marks high on the tin-sheathed poles that supported it. A big bear. It had spooked the dogs out of their appetites, so it must have been a damn big bear. But the snow had obscured most of its sign. I kept a rifle handy just in case it was still around.

The cabin was cold and dreary without Josey. I fired up the stoves, but even at full blaze it still felt chilly. After unloading the supplies I'd picked up in Anchorage with Mister Fong's two hundred, I unchained the dogs and wrestled them into their harnesses, then took them on a long, leg-stretching run down the Alugiak for an hour, letting them work the stagnation and fear out of their systems. And my own. I didn't like this business with the tusks, but it was the only thing I could do if we were to build the lodge and make our way in the hunting business. Anchorage had left me with a sour belly. I could feel those snakes squirming in there, and that night I slept poorly despite the run. I dreamed of Doctor Moran, his bony hand on Josey's breast. Vassily Volkov and Mister Fong were playing Chinese checkers on top of the glacier. Charlie Blue came lumbering toward them dressed all in hides, growling hideously through yellow teeth. Josey screamed but it was only the dogs howling. Howling down the moon.

In the morning I slept late, then dawdled over breakfast. I spent more time meticulously watering Josey's houseplants and herbs, though they looked healthy and pert despite my absence. I gathered together the bone saw, a heavy-spined fleshing knife and a pry bar. Then I took down Josey's Mannlicher carbine and loaded it with five rounds of 220-grain soft points, brazen fingers of death, each of which delivered nearly a ton and a half of knockdown energy at pointblank range. If the visitor were still around and proved to be a brown bear, weighing in at fifteen hundred pounds, rather than a grizzly half that heft, I should be armed powerfully enough to stop him. I doubted, though, that a brown would stray this far from the coast.

Yet why should the dogs be so craven? Normally, they put on a bold front when we came upon grizzly sign, growling and raising their ruffs, sniffing the big tracks or the steaming mounds of dung as if to say "Lemme at him, Boss!" Even Ulf, the big, black, somber-eyed leader, normally the most confident of dogs, seemed to prefer the protection of the cabin crawl space to a walk in the woods with Daddy. I unsnapped him anyway and took him with me. He would spot the bear before I could, and even if he bolted back toward the cabin, I would have time to get the rifle up.

The trail to the glacier wound through heavy willow brake along the Alugiak, an old game run, but the new-fallen snow obscured any footprints more than a day old. I brushed a few drifts clear, down to the old snow, but could see no sign. The bear probably gave up when he couldn't climb the slippery poles to the cache and headed off looking for an old wolf kill to ease the hunger of his long sleep. Ulf still seemed wary, though, hanging back and marking every treetrunk with a cocked leg, or else studying the branches overhead as if he expected a red squirrel to drop out into his jaws. Then, as I was stooping my way under an arch of snow-freighted willow suckers, Ulf gave me the slip. I thought I could hear him crashing off to my left and figured he had probably jumped a snowshoe hare. At least he hadn't spooked back to the cabin.

Once out of the willows, I breathed easier, feeling silly for having worried so much over old bear sign. Out on the scree slope, I could see in all directions. And if the bear appeared, he would spot me at a long enough range for him to alter his vague options. Ninety-nine times out of a hundred—maybe more—a bear will give wide berth to a man. It is only when you surprise him up close, along a brush-choked game trail or a narrow mountainside path, that he finds himself with no choice but to attack. A sow with cubs is another matter, but I had seen only the pawprints of a lone adult at the cache.

When I reached the mouth of the ice passage, I leaned the rifle against a boulder. . . .

It would be ready to hand when I came out. . . .

If the bear was waiting. . . .

CHAPTER SIXTEEN

*A*S HE was, in the ice chamber, eating Doctor Moran.

At first, I mistook the crackling sound for the rasp of my boots on the slick sides of the tunnel. But when I reached the smooth, sturdy tusks and no longer had to skid myself upward, all elbows and knees, I thought perhaps it was my breathing that caused the harsh, echoing *râle,* or maybe the edge of the bone saw sliding across the ice. I suppose the sound of his own teeth working frozen flesh masked the noise of my approach. At any event, we surprised one another.

I was climbing toward two tusks that protruded near the top of the tunnel. Their absence, when I'd sawed them free, wouldn't prevent us from climbing up there later. They were fully exposed, with only the hairy gums of the mammoth who owned them locked back in thin ice. I planned to chisel with the pry bar until I could cut into the animal's jawbone and remove as much tusk as possible; at forty bucks a pound, the effort would be worthwhile.

My mind, I must shamefully admit, was on how I would delude Josey, if she indeed returned. I would head for Anchorage with my ivory, make the swap with Mister Fong (taking due precaution that he not outnumber me and acquire the ivory at pistol point, sans greenbacks—Healey had told me too many tales of oriental mischief to leave me vulnerable on that score). Then I would fly up to Taklavik where the Dewline boys played poker. I'd blow a bit of the money on a couple of nights' worth of cards, then up the ante until I'd won a decent-sized pot. Maybe two or three grand. The way the popsicle grapevine worked, that sum would treble by the time the word reached Anchorage, quintuple at Gurry Bay.

Not only would I be lucky at cards, I'd beat the odds and luck out at love as well.

I slid over the lip of the cavern's mouth and the pry bar clanked on the ice. Something went whuff. A cloud sloped away from the sun and the light came in strong, easing the darkness from squid-ink blue to a hollow, cathedral mauve. He was standing, hunched, with a clot of black spaghetti dangling from his jaws—Doctor Moran's frozen guts, the liver pendant—all eight foot of him, silver-blue in the passing light, puzzled at the intrusion. A glacier bear. The biggest I'd ever seen.

Something strange happens when you're in that close to a creature more alien than death. His stink—moldy cave, frozen thighs, fear and rage—smells sensible, predictable; it matches your own. I could almost see his balls shrink back into his belly as I felt my own shrivel. He rattled his teeth in synchrony with mine and I could feel waves of rage and fear pour off of him, hot and fetid, flight and fight, as if we had grown the same glands and the same speedy legs and the same claws and teeth (if it came to that). We were fuck fighting scared.

With no way out.

I think we realized it, each in his own way, at the same moment. If I dived down the chute, he'd be right after me. If he dived down the chute, he'd carry me with him, squalling like a newborn lamb.

If I had the rifle, I'd have plugged him where he stood, burst my eardrums in the process, and then taken the dive.

If he'd had the rifle he'd have chewed it like licorice.

All of this took but a flash, three fast heartbeats, a single fart (from him). Then he came down on all fours and charged.

Most of this (like my face) is a reconstruction. He must have hit me head to belly, bowling me backward down the chute, the two of us rattling across the bars of ivory like madmen playing *Chopsticks*, my ribs popping while his merely bent and bruised, him bawling and chuffing in that deep ugly way they have when they're frightened or hard hit by a big bullet, claws rattling against the ice and around my ears, the stink of his winter-rancid hair in my face (I hugged him as I'd never hugged Josey, tight around the neck, my nose in his armpit) all the time gone and only the blue rapids of ice beneath and around and within us, until we hit bottom.

Whuff. Again. From both of us.

But his rage was more complete than mine. His nervous system, simpler in the realities, sent him back onto me, arms slapping and grabbing as Gainey's had, so ineffectively, on Sam. Then his right paw taking my head behind the neck and stuffing it, eyes first, into his wide mouth. I felt his tongue on my chin, like a hot towel in a barbershop, his claws forcing my skull into that gap, the two of us spinning and whirling, over and over down the scree, the slime of Doctor Moran's guts thawing in my nostrils, and I forced my left arm up into the gap between his molars, taking the brunt of his bite on my forearm.

I could feel—I remember it clearly, and the scars will prove me true—the raking locking touch of his canines on the back of my skull. I heard my head pop like a pecan in a nutcracker. And I remembered the first and only rule that applies when you're being mauled by a bear.

Play dead.

I went limp as a brainshot wolf. Tried not to breathe (try it sometime when you have to). Let him bat and chaw some more—arm, foot, shoulder. Heard him huffing hard, smelled his stink, through my slitted eyes saw the mass of him, shag against the hard blue sky, fleas crawling on his slack belly, my own blood matting his clacking, foamy jaws. His eyes looked away from me—good. He figured me finished. Slowly I felt his rage subside, and faster than that the sting of the wounds he'd paid me for my rude intrusion.

He wandered off, I think.

I slept.

When I woke, he was off at the edge of the scree slope, whacking at a rotted blowdown, hoping, I guess, for maggots.

The Mannlicher was ten yards away, at best.

Yet, if he stayed that way, his back toward me. . . . If his rage was indeed blown from the fight. . . .

I could only see out of my right eye. Maybe he was closer. Maybe I was dead.

My knees worked. My elbows. The adrenalin was still up so that the pain lay perhaps ten minutes in the future. The rifle was closer.

When I moved, he chuffed and stood up, ears cocked, eyes focusing that long long way to where I lay. Maybe twenty yards.

He ran toward me with a kind of chortling, whuffling grin on his face, then spun around on his haunches and scratched himself with his right hind leg. He licked his paw. He rubbed his ass on the gravel. He ambled back down to the log.

I crawled toward the rifle, inch at a time, minutes between inches, aches turning to stabs, stabs to saw cuts. Time was running out.

He came up the slope in that late light, blue now in the setting sun, and hit me once or twice with his right paw—the one he'd licked for my blood. He grabbed me by the shoulder, carefully, with his jaws and lifted me up and shook me. I stayed limp. My head shook. My jaws clattered. My tongue lolled. I rolled my eyes back into my head. Dead as he could ever wish.

He dragged me toward a stack of brush, winterkilled runoff brush at the edge of the Alugiak, then thought better of it. Question: Do grizzly bears understand spring runoff?

Probably. When the river rose at breakup, it would sluice his rotten tidbit away.

He carried me back up to the cave mouth and flopped me down within arm's reach of the Mannlicher. Then he waddled off down the scree slope, figuring maybe to stow me later, up in the ice cave, where he'd eaten the good Doctor Moran.

My arms still worked, though slowly. I took the rifle down

from its leaning perch on the ice-scrubbed rock. I saw him down there, at his log again, heavy back humped silver in the last light, the long-nosed snipy face in profile, and laid the sights on his ear. He was chewing like a dog on a deer leg.

I blew his brains down into the snow.

The shock of the recoil against my dislocated shoulder opened the floodgates and the pain came crashing down on me so that the whole world thinned and went white and I could see millions of tiny bright particles shooting at me from the horizon fast as the speed of light and the stones themselves went porous. When it all came together again, the sun was nearly gone. Where the bear had fallen over the rotting log I saw a raven, bobbing its head at me, its eyes bright as it chortled deep in its throat. I could not see the bear. The raven spread its wings, puffed the feathers on its throat, and flapped off into the dusk.

How I made it back to the cabin I do not know. I have vague, perhaps imagined, memories of sliding on my side through cold mud, and of Ulf emerging from the dark to whine and lick at the blood on my face, and perhaps he grabbed my collar and helped me drag myself along. Nor do I know how I managed to rig the noose over the ridgepole in the cabin and slip the hand of my dislocated arm into it, and then throw my whole weight downward in an effort to snap the head of the humerus back in its socket. But it worked. When I came to, dangling from the rope, my shoulder once more could flex.

Later, I found that half the bottle of codeine pills we kept for emergencies was missing, so I must have eaten them. I recall trying to drink a glass of brandy to ease the pain, but the liquid slopped out of the sides of my mouth. My jaw hung down on my chest. Then I remembered Josey's basting tube with the suction bulb on the end. I blasted my glottis with brandy and water and made my way to bed.

Perhaps a kind of subliminal shock wave rolls out from the epicenter of a wilderness calamity, or maybe it's just the gathering of carrion eaters, but miles and miles away up Carcajou Creek, Charlie Blue knew I was in trouble. I heard him singing and whooping long before the hiss of his sled runners announced his arrival. For days, it seemed, I had lain there in the slow wash and ebb of fever, broken and stiff and half blind, crawling the few feet to the stove only when the cabin's chill set my hot skin to aching, boiling up a can of pea soup or tomato soup, sucking it down through the baster, stoking the fire, while the dogs howled and the wolves joined their chorus from the hills beyond the ice.

I heard his footsteps on the stoop.

"Strange," he hollered. "No smoke from the chimney, yet the airplane is parked on the river. No sound from within, yet the dogs are silent. No sign in the snow, yet the ravens gather as if to eat."

I mumbled something through my broken jaw.

"What's that? An animal inside the cabin. A wolf? A lynx? Surely not a bear." I heard him lever a round into his battered .300 Savage. I mumbled louder, trying to call his name.

The door opened and the muzzle of the rifle peeked in. Half delirious, I half hoped he would plug me and put me out of my pain. Then his hooded head eased around the doorframe and he peered into the darkness. He sniffed.

"Hmm," he yelled, "smells of blood and shit. Someone's been cooking pea soup." I mumbled again, unable to articulate, and he ducked back, slamming the door. For a long while, I heard him conducting a learned dialogue with himself as he sat on the porch, debating what could be causing the noises within. Then at last he hit it. "Aha! Slade is in there! He is hurt! He cannot speak, so he mumbles! What could have hurt him so badly? A bear."

I heard him walking away from the cabin, probably to look for the signs of the fight. I slept for a while, and then I heard him returning. This time he came right into the cabin. Took the brandy bottle from the shelf and uncorked it. Glug glug. Then he lit the kerosene lamp.

"Poor Slade," he said.

By the time Josey returned four days later, he had patched me up pretty well. He stitched my torn scalp and poulticed it with moss and lichens. He bound my cracked ribs with torn sheets. He rearticulated my jaw with powerful fingers and sewed up the slashes the bear's teeth had left in my thigh, my shoulder and my face. He cooked for me and fed me, cleaned me with hot water, made me get up and work the stiffness out of my wounds and my muscles. He forced me to drink herbal infusions that eased my fever. And all the while, he sang. It was driving me nuts.

I heard an aircraft motor circling overhead, and the splash and revs of the landing, the grating of floats on gravel. Only then did I realize that breakup had come and gone. I must have been delirious when the ice went out, although I do recall strange dreams in which the roar and rumble of ice played a prominent part. Josey's footsteps sounded on the stoop and Charlie led her in.

"Oh God, Jack," she said, looking at me. "Oh God."

Behind her loomed another figure, black against the lighted doorway. It was Sam Healey.

"I don't know about you, honey," he said, "but I think it makes him look prettier."

PART TWO

SAM HEALEY

1980

CHAPTER SEVENTEEN

BUT GOD he was a mess. His head looked the size of a basketball, and lines of black stitches zigzagged across his scalp, down his forehead and over his left cheekbone. His left eye was puffed shut and he never would regain full vision in it. His nose was broken and his jaw hung crooked and there was a deep slash across his throat, stitched up by the Indian now, but from then on he would talk in a hoarse whisper, like some racetrack tout with a hot tip or a stumblebum asking for a handout. We tried to cheer him up. Old Jack was tough all right.

The girl was something else. Not much of a looker in my book and a real Goody Two-Shoes in many ways, but she was clearly head over heels, changing his bandages, plumping his pillow, feeding him tea and soup, sitting next to him when he slept so that if his fever came back she could lay cold compresses on his torn head. I'd picked her up in Gurry Bay. She'd been Outside, she said, to bury her mother. My pardon came through, finally, and I'd flown in from Juneau with the company plane to see the old gang and find out how Jack was faring.

After the dustup on the dock, I'd made a beeline for the Canuck border, put down in Whitehorse, and sold the Dakota to a couple of guys who planned to head down to South America and see what was happening air-freight-wise. Then I lined up a job roughnecking at an oil camp near Norman Wells in the Northwest Territories. Under a phony monicker, naturally. The outfit was Morgan Petroleum, Jep Morgan's show, just getting under way in the business that would ultimately make him the biggest independent north of the border.

Jep was a long drink from Louisiana, a big, hamhanded, walnut-faced redneck with an eye for the main chance. He'd come out of the Marines a bird colonel after the war and made a killing in cheap housing. He wanted to get into the oil game down home but all the good leases were sewed up tight, so with the dough from his ticky-tack developments, he headed north and began wildcatting there in the tundra. He hit a couple of good wells and sold them off to the big companies, and with the money from that he started expanding. By the time I got to know him, he had four rigs, two canneries, ten salmon seiners, a small logging company in Southeast, half a dozen whorehouses up and down the coast from British Columbia to Nome, and lots of political clout in Juneau. My kind of guy.

In those early days, Jep still catted around with the crew, played a lot of guts poker and slugged back the hooch with both fists. He liked his nookie. Thanks to my bush flying experience, I knew every worthwhile split-tail in the North and fixed him up with some good stuff. I let him know I was on the lam and that I was a damn good flier. Pretty soon, I was his personal pilot and he went to bat for me with the law on the Olds charge. Things were pretty loose back then, and it was easy enough to fix.

As luck would have it, Jep had a marriageable daughter, Ellen, kind of an ugly duckling, like her dad, but shy and awkward. It was a cinch to get into her pants. For real fucking, I like 'em dim and dirty but good looking. This twist was none of the above, but she was bloody rich. The only reason to marry.

I filled Jack in on this one afternoon as we sat on the gravel bar watching the Alugiak flush past, full of grit and the last chunks of the winter's ice. It was warm but the flies weren't out yet. Josey was out back chopping firewood and Jack lay on a mattress she'd hauled out there for him. His bruises had gone kind of a dirty yellow green and his puffed eye was opening, glinting in there out of focus. Charlie Blue was gone, God knows where.

"I'm glad you're doing okay, pal," he croaked.

"What the hell," I said. "*We're* doing okay, partner. We're still partners, you know. Soon as I get back to town, I'll send you up a check for your share of what I got for the Dakota, a couple of grand anyway. And now that I'm with Morgan, I can steer a lot of business your way, hauling gear and people to Jep's drill sites."

"No," he says, "I'm through with flying for a living. I want to turn this place into a good hunting camp. Maybe with that dough, I can get a leg up on it. Anyways, with this goddam walleye the bear gave me, I'd never get my commercial license back."

"Well, if it's hunting, shit, I can help you out there too. We've got a lot of wild-ass Texans who love to hunt. Krauts too, rich ones, and a few Arabs. Big money there. But you'll have to fix the place up nice and comfortable for them."

The shack they lived in was a dump. You could see he'd socked it together without any professional help. They didn't even have electricity or an indoor can. How the hell the twist managed to pee during the winter without growing icicles on her pussy, I'll never know. Maybe she did. Jack wouldn't know the difference.

"You'll need separate cabins where they can bring in their ginch, and a big fireplace for them to loll around at night and swap lies. A long bar like Norman Ormandy has in the Blue Bear. Lots of stuff."

"Yeah," he says, "well I haven't got the money for that. I had a plan to get some but I thought better of it."

"Money's no problem," I tell him. I'm getting excited now, I can see it all taking shape. "I'm sure I can sell Jep on the idea. A special hunting camp for his rich-bitch pals in the oil business. Fly 'em here in the Bonanza, loaded for bear.

You line 'em up with big trophies, I line 'em up with some of my cuties. A great working vacation."

He looks at me with that weird eye, like some kind of evil hairy toad.

"If I do it," he says, "they'll work for their meat. I'm not staking out targets for them. I don't want any slob hunting here. Fair chase or no chase."

"Sure," I said. I guessed we could work that out when and if. Anyway, he was still punchy from the bear whacking him around. He'd come to his senses when the money was whistling in.

"Another thing," he croaks, "Josey."

"What about her?"

"I don't want her becoming just a chief cook and bottle washer. If we're to do this right, we'll need a regular staff, a chef and sous-chef, people to clean up and chop firewood, a couple of wranglers for the horses, some good hunters—pros—to back me up. Would your guy Morgan go for that?"

"I think I can sell it," I told him.

"What kind of money we talking about?"

"I'll have to work that out with Morgan."

That night after dinner—Josey had a touch, I'll admit, at least with wild meat—I knew they wanted to talk so I took a rod and went down to Carcajou Creek to try for some trout. Ulf, their big Husky, came with me to keep a lookout for bears.

There wasn't much action so I circled in behind the cabin and looked for that oil seep I'd spotted when we were forced down on the glacier. It was still there—I could smell it a hundred yards away—and from what I'd learned about oil in the NWT I had a feeling that this could be a seep from a big pool. It would be another selling point as far as Jep was concerned. He always had his eye out for new ground. Slade and I were into this homestead thing fifty-fifty, equal partners, and once I'd arranged the deal with Morgan to develop the place as a hunting camp, he'd be in debt to me. When the time came to make use of the oil rights, he'd be bounden, unable to say no. All the more reason to cave in to his whims. Why the hell did that bitch need a chef and a sous-chef?

When I got back to the cabin, I could hear them talking

about the deal. Okay, I'm an eavesdropper, always have been, but how else do you really learn what your friends are thinking?

"You call him your friend," she was saying, "but he left you holding the bag in Gurry Bay. You could have been convicted for that. You lost your license over it anyway. What kind of a friend is that?"

Jack mumbled something I didn't catch, but I heard her sniff. What a ballbuster! I bet her cunt was lined with sandpaper right then.

"Okay, so you'll have full charge. Fair chase. Fine. But remember what you said about Outside? You'll be inviting Outside in."

"Only for a little while," he said.

"You tried it the other way," she yipped, "and now you want to try it this way. Neither of them will work."

Grumble-scrape-grunt, from Jack.

"I don't understand you."

"Look, this is what I want more than anything," he grates. "Nearly anything."

"What else?"

"I want us to be married, and for you to stop worrying about if I can handle this, and let me be your husband and take care of things."

There's a long, long silence and I can hear her padding back and forth on the planks in her mukluks.

"Maybe so," she says finally. "I told you before I wasn't ready for it, but it looks like now I am." Her voice is gone softer now, kind of little-girl wheedling, the way they do when they got you where they want you.

"How do you mean?"

"Pregnant." And she laughs.

I knew I had him.

CHAPTER EIGHTEEN

*S*O SLADE had his way. How many men can look back over a quarter of a century and say they led precisely the life they wished? He certainly could, though now the goddam ingrate is out there somewhere plotting our destruction. Still, can I blame him? After all, I did betray him, though I'm sure he knew I was planning it all along.

Look at all we gave him. Even while he was recovering from the mauling by the bear, work gangs from Morgan Petro's MorgArctic Construction subsidiary were hard at work expanding his dinky cabin into a fine, sprawling lodge, built of well-cured prefab cedar from Wisconsin. They installed generators and electricity, lights and freezers and refrigerators. They dug septic tanks and lay hundreds of feet of pipe. They drove a well more than two hundred feet down into that permafrost and brought in sparkling clear water with no glacial sediment in it to grind down your teeth and clog your bowels. They fenced in a huge corral and threw up a horse barn to house the two dozen pack and riding horses provided, free of charge, by Jep Morgan, along with a gang of crack Texas and Montana wranglers to handle the herd.

While all this was going on, Jep sent Jack and Josey off to Hawaii for a free honeymoon vacation at the Kailua-Kona Inn on the big island. Jack went out deep-sea fishing every day and caught a 680-pound blue marlin. Jep paid to have it mounted, and the fish hangs to this day over the mantle in the main lodge's rec room, along with dozens of other trophies—moose, caribou, sheep, mountain goat—taken by Jack and his hunting clients over the years. Not a penny did he have to pay for the mounting of those heads.

Of course, while the Slades were off honeymooning, we flew in a gang of doodlebugs to run a seismic survey of the area. For the better part of a month, the jug hustlers laid out their geophones in a cross-hatched series of survey lines, drilling crews bored holes for the charges, and the woods echoed to the pow of the shooter's blasts. The head geophysicist plotted the echoes and confirmed, as we'd all expected, that there was indeed an anticline under the glacier—a dome of unruptured rock beneath which lay a reservoir of oil and natural gas. The presence of the oil seeps—we found three others, in addition to the one that had first tipped me to the possibility—made it seem likely that the reservoir was a big one. The trick would be to tap it without disturbing the glacier.

"That's a tetchy sumbitch," Jep said, staring up at the ice one afternoon. "We'll have to drill in directionally, down at an angle from this side of the ice. The geo guys say it's not more'n five thousand feet to the anticline, then maybe another thousand to get through it. Burn up a few bits when we get down there, I reckon."

"You're not going in right away?" I asked him.

"Naw," he said. "Like we planned, we'll hold this un in reserve. Right now, with the cost of cutting a road in here from the coast to lug out the crude, plus the cost of bringing in the rig and all, it wouldn't be worth it. But mark my words, Sammy boy, there'll come a time when all of that *will* pay. Right now it seems we got the Ay-rabs eating out of our hands. But you look at that long-snouted cunnel in Egypt, Camel Nasser or whatever they call him, he's up to no good as far as we and the limeys are concerned. And there'll be more like him ere long."

So the plan remained as we'd first discussed it—without Jack's knowledge, of course. We'd build up the game lodge, use it to entertain Jep's many business contacts, make what money we could from it by letting only the wealthiest of American and European hunters—serious hunters, sheep men and bear men—hunt with Jack when we weren't using the place. And then, when the price was right, we'd break the news to Jack-O. We needed his signature to secure the mineral rights in their entirety.

Still, he must have known it was coming, sooner or later.

Jack and Jep hit it off quite well together. Out back of his office in Juneau, Jep had built an obstacle course complete with rope swings, high board walls, stake-lined ditches, and a big traverse of monkey bars socked together out of peeled logs. It was his custom to run every new employee over the course to see if he was fit to be hired. Jep had a pair of English pit bulls—Rip and Rumble, he called them—and he would give the new would-be Morganite a thirty-second start over the dogs (who actually were too clumsy to catch any man in reasonable condition). When Jack was healthy again after the bear, he came down to Juneau on some business and Jep asked him to try the course.

"You gonna sic them dogs on me?" Jack asked him.

"That's the plan."

"How highly you value them?"

"Cost me two hundred apiece," says Jep.

"Take it out of my this year's pay."

Jack lopes out onto the course and vaults the first fence, then saunters toward the trench filled with sharpened bamboo stakes. This you were supposed to cross on a rope swing. He waits until the dogs have scrabbled over the fence and are huffing toward him, their piggy red little eyes gleaming and their long crocodile snouts snapping in anticipation of a hunk of human haunch. Then he swings out over the spikes, only about three quarters of the way, swings back in and kicks Rip in the nose. The dog leaps at Jack's feet as he swings back over the pit. Rip plunges out of sight—yipe!

Rumble is smarter, though. Even from where we stood we could see the light flick on in his eyes. He circles the stake pit and waits for Jack on the far side. Jack hand-for-hands up the rope to the beam that supports it, then tightwires his way so that he's standing over the dog. He's wearing heavy logger's boots.

"Bombs away!" he yells.

Splat. Right on old Rumble's guts. Rumble uttered a final fart, then was no more.

Jack jogs the rest of the way through the course in the slowest time any employee ever recorded.

"Am I hired?"

"Hell, boy," says Jep between wheezy guffaws, "you always *was* hired. This was just fer fun."

Both of them were crack shots with both rifle and shotgun. Jep built a skeet range behind the lodge and the two of them shot there every time Jep came up. After a while that got boring, so Jep started shooting the clays with a .22 rifle. Jack one-upped him with a pistol. Then Jep appeared with a pair of crossbows. On doubles he'd take one with his right hand, the next with his left. Jack thought of moving down to a slingshot, but said to hell with it.

One spring, after the runoff had abated to fast water and only a few small ice floes, Jep showed up with a couple of wetsuits and a hankering for a swim. "Race ya to the jam," he tells Jack.

About two miles downstream from the lodge, there was a colossal tangle of piled up ice and uprooted trees blocking the river just above the Mad Wolf Rapids, a stretch of skookumchuck (strong water, in Indian talk) that at this season was a sheer half mile of boiling death. The ice jam had it half tamed right now, but the minute it went out all hell would break loose. Jack looks at the river and then up at the sky for a minute—it was one of those spring days so hot it could frizzle a side of salmon in the sun, but with ice lying back in heaps under the trees.

"Can't accommodate you this morning, Boss," Jack croaks in that sarcastic way of his. "Got some chores that won't wait. But how's about this afternoon, on about happy hour?"

I saw him ride out of camp a little while later on one of the cayuses, with a packed saddlebag and a coil of wire. I figured he was going up to one of the nearby spike camps to refence the corral.

He was back in time for the big swim meet, though. The two of them wriggled into their black rubber suits—Jep's had a yellow hood on it so I could tell them apart as I followed them in the outboard—and waded out into the shallows. The water was mucky brown with slivers of ice spinning in the eddies but neither of them yelped or shivered. I gave them their start, with a .44 revolver.

They lunged out into the current and I scrambled into the outboard to follow. The motor wouldn't start until the third yank on the cord, so by the time I caught up with them, they were already a quarter mile downstream, with Jep in the lead, turning on his back now and then to whoop back at Jack and flag him on. They swept through the bends like seals after salmon, shouldering the ice floes aside and staying to the main current. The speed was incredible, even when viewed from the outboard, and the trees along the bank spun by like bike spokes, lit by that low white-hot sun. Eagles spooked off the snags and magpies squalled.

Then they came around the final bend above the jam. The ice and mangled sweepers stood like a blue-black wall against the horizon, jumbled and packed every which way, groaning at the weight of dirty brown water pressed against it, popping occasionally as a tree or a floe cracked to the river's push. Beyond it you could hear the low grumble of the skookumchuck. The jam had formed a huge turbid lake of slow water this side of it, and ice rafts circled in the swirl of the water. They entered this temporary lake nearly together, with Jep holding onto a body-length lead and stroking loose and easy in a heads-up crawl.

Then I saw Jack cut toward the bank, sprinting. What the hell was this? Old Jack-Off quitting? But I saw he was headed for a big sweeper that stuck out from the bank, a great old spruce that had been undercut by the runoff and now lay angled into the stream with its black-clad limbs flopping in the water like some giant squid covered with short hair. Jep had turned and spotted what Jack was up to. He treaded water and watched.

Jack scrambled up onto the sweeper and picked something out of a crotch in the branches. It was an exploder box. The water dripped off the wire that led into the river angling down in the direction of the ice jam.

"Hey, Jep," he shouts. "Let's finish with a real kick!" He pulls up the handle of the plunger, then socks it home.

Wham! The whole middle of the ice jam rose up into the air like a cat hunching its back. Brown water and a sky full of spinning, splintering sticks, whole slabs of ice whirling off like the chunks of a shattered clay pigeon. The water went out into the skookumchuck with a sucking, rattling rush, and the spruce Jack was standing on wrenched free of the bank and spun out into the main current. Jack reached out as it passed Jep and yanked him up onto the trunk. The tree and its riders swirled down into the rapids, and as it disappeared into the dirty spray, I could hear the two of them yelling, Jack in his crazy raven's croak and Jep like a goddam bronco buster.

I roared back up to the lodge at full speed, feeling a bit shaky and with that hollow feeling in the gut when you know something awful is happening and you can't stop it. Josey was waiting on the dock as I pulled up.

"What happened?"

I pushed past her and ran to where the Supercub was moored to the bar, cast off and slid in behind the stick. She started on the first turn of the prop and I didn't even bother to check the instruments or the wind, just jammed full throttle into her and skipped over the ice and the water, popped a float clear, then the other and banked downstream at treetop level.

From the air, the skookumchuck looked uglier than it had sounded on the water. Whitehorses of tan and gray and pinto black spewing and puking down through the big black rocks that stuck like broken teeth out of the foam. No way they could have lived through that rush. I climbed to three hundred feet and sinuated downstream, looking for signs of their broken bodies. The black of the wetsuits, and particularly Jep's yellow hood, ought to stick out in the gray-brown suds that lined the shore.

About five miles downstream, I found them.

Sitting on the end of a little island, whooping and waving up at me.

Jep had a silver flask of Wild Turkey in his paw, that he'd carried in the wetsuit to celebrate the end of the race. By the time I'd landed and taxied up to them, they were shitfaced, the both of them, with only a little blood oozing out of cuts on their faces and out of the tattered, floppy black shreds that had been their wetsuits.

CHAPTER NINETEEN

THE BEAR must have done a job on Jack's balls, gave
him a crude vasectomy or something, because they only had
the one kid. It was a boy, John Strong Slade, Junior, but when
he got older everyone called him Dude. Like his dad, he was
short but wiry tough and he had a way with animals, wild
and tame, like no one I've ever known. Particularly horses.
He could hardly walk yet when Jack had him up on the back
of one of the remuda, and he was throwing a rope like a
veteran by the time he was five. The wranglers loved him
and taught him all their tricks and he got so that he could
bust a hardnosed new bronc in a dozen jumps, and not with
a lot of heavy stuff, quirt and spurs and Spanish bits, but
just by letting the pony know he would not come off. The
wranglers fitted him out with tiny chaps and hand-tooled boots
and a Stetson you could of boiled muskrat in, and that's how
he got the name Dude.

He knew where every moose and bear and caribou in the
country hung out and he got so he could take you to them,
pussyfooting along on horseback so that you were on them

before they knew it. He claimed he could talk to bears and always felt bad when someone plugged one, but that didn't keep him from wolfing down the meat when it came suppertime. He always had a pet raven riding on his shoulder or the pommel of his saddle, and for a long while, he had a pet golden eagle named Skraw who ate raw meat from his hand and killed ground squirrels for Dude to feed to his other pets of the moment—weasels, skunks, lynxes and coyotes. Down at the mouth of the river, in wetsuit, fins and goggles, he swam with the sea otters and the hair seals, watching them fish and winning their confidence so that some days you could see him up on the rocks with them, sunning together, Dude as black and shiny in his wetsuit as any seal.

Jack and I dove with him a few times. It was eerie down there in the dark blue cold, weaving your way through the thick yellow rubbery stalks of kelp, with the sunlight slanting in low through the clouds of microlife that thicken the waters of the Gulf to a copepod soup, and when Dude's favorite seal slipped up behind me and suddenly popped its head over my shoulder, its whiskers beaded with little air bubbles and its eyes bulging into my face plate, I like to croaked right there. Another time we swam with the sea lions. The big bulls would come charging straight at you, their foreheads domed like the heads of earless Labrador retrievers, and then whip into a ponderous barrel roll that would take them past so fast and big you could feel the pulse of the water they displaced pushing you sideways.

"When they come at you like that," Dude said, "don't for the life of you try to duck aside. You might duck into their path. Then it's splat, so long."

Dude found a cave back in along the cliffs. You had to dive down about twenty feet and then snake your way in through a winding passageway another forty feet or so, and then you came up into a dimly lit cavern behind the rock wall. Up at the top the light came in faintly and the air column in the cave rose and fell, hooting as it was expelled through the chimney. The first we learned of it was one day when Dude was about twelve or thirteen and we were all down at the river mouth for a picnic. Jack and Josey and my old lady and I were in the Zodiac raft while Dude and my daughter, Susan, dived for abalone and crab. The two kids got on great together, practically grew up summers in the same skin, and Suzy was nearly as good in the water as Dude, though she couldn't stay down as long. They had been diving along the cliff wall when suddenly Josey says, "My God, where are they?"

The two women are up on their feet, bouncing the raft around like it would tip, and then panicking one another, unable to spot the kids' heads through the low chop that had sprung up. They were deathly afraid of killer whales, though Dude said he often swam with them in clear water and they paid no attention to him. Jack and I are trying to calm the ladies down and sneaking looks at one another and working hard to keep ourselves from screaming when we hear this weird, hollow howl—like a giant wolfpack singing the moon. The howl has two notes to it, low and grainy, high and screechy—and they weave back and forth together into the most doleful, cold, heartsick sound you ever heard.

"What is it, what is it?" squeals Ellie, my old lady.

"I'm going in there," croaks Jack, stripping off his shirt and pants and grabbing up a spare face mask.

Then we hear the howl turn to laughter. It's the kids, back in the cave, as they told us later. Of course there's nothing for it but Jack must go in there himself and see the sights, and I with him so as not to look chicken in front of my family, but I never liked it back in that cave, never for a second, not the going in or the howling or the coming out with the rocks scraping on belly and butt and the air tight in your lungs and not knowing what or who will be waiting with its mouth open on the far end.

Like most kids who grow up in Alaska, Dude was a demon with machinery. He could tear down and put together any motor ever made, or build one out of spare parts with only a minimum of tools. He knew how to fly the Cessna before he could spell the word, and he drove a log skidder like a grownup before he was twelve. He was always good with big gear—graders, Cats, shovels, dump trucks—better by far than Jack or any of us, and he never could swallow the irony of child labor laws that prevented him from going out to work his skills when men older but dead stupid when it came to machinery could kill themselves and others on any job in the state. "It's not fair," he would holler. "I'm better than those jerks and I need money too!" He wanted to buy a thirty-foot double-ender ketch he'd seen in Valdez and sail out to the Tuamotus in the South Pacific. He'd been reading Jack London. He had just turned fourteen.

That was the summer he and Suzy ran away. I was Outside on business for Morgan when it happened but Ellie was up at the lodge with Jack and Josey. The way Jack told it, he woke up one morning and they were gone, with just the canoe and a couple of rifles and some camp gear, plus a submersible gas-powered dredge and a small sluice box Dude had welded out of old scrap. "Since I can't get a job in town," he wrote in the note he'd left on the kitchen wall, "I'm taking Suzy with me and we're going for gold. It's a stream I found long ago that has good color in it and you won't be able to find it so don't come looking for us. I know what I'm doing and can take care of us okay and *I want that boat!* Your loving son, Johnnie." He never called himself Dude in those days, would punch you in the Adam's apple if you said it to his face. Very feisty.

A few years later, the teenage runaway would become a commonplace figure in American society, what with the Haight-Ashbury and all, but Jack at least took it calmly. "I've trusted my own life to that kid," he said, "out in the woods or up in the mountains or underwater amongst the killer whales. He'll be okay." The mothers, though, were frantic, Josey less so than Ellie, I must admit, and they finally talked me into flying a search for them. I suspect Jack knew all along what creek they were on, he knew every slough and trickle in the Dead Mountie range, and surely the old Indian, Charlie Blue, who lived nearly full time at the lodge now as a tracker, wrangler and general factotum, knew where they were, but the two of them played dumb.

I flew the country on and off for the better part of two weeks, with one or the other of the ladies serving as extra eyes, but we couldn't find a trace of them—not a tendril of campsmoke, not a streak of discolored water in the creeks from their dredge. Now and then we would see figures in the streams and I would swoop down in the Bonanza with

Ellie or Josey whiteknuckled beside me, but inevitably it would turn out bears or moose. There were a lot of bears that summer but I was less concerned with them than I was with Dude's pecker.

"He's balling that girl," I told Ellie more than once. "That little diddler, when they come back I'll kick his ass good. If he's got her pregnant . . ."

"Don't worry about it," my good wife said. "She's a decent girl and she wouldn't do anything like that."

"Why not? You sure as hell did."

We never got on too well, Ellie and I. She was a bulb-nosed, lank-haired, big-hipped ballbuster and she knew I'd married her for her father's money. How the girl ever came out looking so good I'll never know. She was leggy and blonde, with fine features and nice, warm brownish-green eyes wide apart, and even when she was little, she had a kind of husky voice, lazy and sensual. I was embarrassed to bounce her on my knee.

"Sure I did," Ellie would say, bitter-like. "Because you begged me to. You said you couldn't live if I didn't. You told me I was beautiful and I believed you, even though the mirror and everybody else showed me otherwise." She had a washed-out voice, that woman. Maybe if she'd had some pep, it would have been different. I've screwed ugly women galore in my time and when they had some pep they could be beautiful, in an odd way, even through their ugliness. But when a woman is a whiner and doesn't have any get-up-and-go, then even the ones with classic kissers are dogs. Suzy, though, she had pep, and so did that bitch Josey. When she was out on the search with me, and it got to midday when the sun cast glaring reflections on the streams and lakes so that you couldn't have seen an elephant drinking down there, she'd make me land on some river or flowage she knew and while I ate my lunch, she'd break out a fishing rod and catch trout until the light got better. Either that or take her Mannlicher and prowl around back in the bush for an hour or so. Now and then I'd hear her shoot, always just the one shot, and soon she'd be back dragging some poor furry critter she'd blasted. Christ, how that woman loved to shoot! And she was good. I never saw her miss, though Jack says that when they first got together she missed a few. Damned if I believe it though. Once—this was not while we were looking for the kids—I was up with her at a camp they had in the Mounties, up in the sheep country, and she and I were sitting outside one afternoon and she says, "Look at that ram."

She's staring out across a deep drop to a cliff half a mile away.

"I don't see anything."

"There on that ledge about three quarters the way up. He's lying down, chewing his cud. He's a full curl if I ever saw one."

She goes in the cabin and brings out her rifle and a pair of binox for me. After about ten minutes I found him, just like she said.

"That's a thousand yards if it's an inch," I told her.

"Wait here."

She slides down over the edge and is gone. About half an hour later, I see her coming up the far side—she must have run down the mountain, that scrawny woman—and she starts plugging up the far side, climbing like a goddam goat. She gets parallel with the ram but she's still a good six, seven hundred yards from him. She's using the boulders to shield her approach but not paying much attention to the rocks she kicks off. Then she takes her rest and, pop, I see the ram slump where he lies.

Two hours later, she's back with the head and the loins, hardly puffing a bit with all that climbing.

"How come he didn't spook when you kicked down all those boulders?" I ask her.

"They're used to hearing rocks fall," she says. "Jack taught me that. They hear it all the time, when weather works stones loose, or bears or other goats or sheep kick them down. They can't smell very keenly either, I guess, because the winds are so variable that it doesn't make much sense for them to panic at every random smell that comes their way. But what they can do like nothing else is see. You have to keep out of their line of sight. Do that, and you've got 'em."

We had mutton chops for dinner that night and if you haven't eaten wild sheep, you haven't eaten. She was a fine cook, that tough broad, and could she shoot. But boy did she hate my guts!

"Why don't you like me, Josey?" I asked her. "Dude likes me fine, and Jack and I have always been close."

"Because you're greedy, Sam," she says. "You see this country as a great big grabbag and all you want to do is take."

"That's the American way," I hold her. "And anyway, what about you and Jack? You're as greedy as I am, in a different way. You want to hold onto your hunk of it and keep it just the way it is. What about all those people Outside who'd give their life savings to spend a summer fishing and hunting or gold-panning up here? I don't see you swinging wide your doors to welcome them. Alaska has riches that the Outside can use, but Alaskans like you and Jack don't want to share. Isn't that greedy?"

It took her aback, I must say. She waffled around for a bit, the color coming up in her cheeks, and then she squares away at me.

"Jack and I believe in taking care of first things first," she says with a huff. "What's most important to us is us, then our friends, and only then the rest of the world. Maybe that's greedy but it's the only priority we can establish."

"Well, then don't call me greedy."

"Don't you go posing as some kind of a goddam altruist, Samuel," she continues, really raging now. "You make it sound like you and Jep Morgan had nothing but the good of the needy Outside at heart. Like hell you do. You want the profits that come from development, and to hell with what's left when you're done. I've seen the cannery towns you've developed, and the mining and oil camps, and the clear cuts where you've logged. It's all of it ugly, uglier than sin. Not a wild animal left in the country. Slag piles and slashings and stinking water, the stink of oil hanging over everything so that the dew falls with a greasy sheen to it. What kind of a world is that?"

"A world with jobs in it for people who want to work, for starters," I say. "Morgan Petro now employs nearly eight thousand people, more than a third of them natives. You and Jack, by the way, have only one native on your staff—Old Charlie. And you're sure as hell the one to sound off like a flower-sniffer. The way you delight in blasting animals and ripping out their guts, you ought to be running a slaughterhouse. I don't think that qualifies you for membership in the Sierra Club or the Friends of Animals."

"Those jerks," she says, flustered and stuttering now. "They've got their heads up—you know where."

I sat back and grinned at her.

"You tell 'em, Josey," I said, "the whole world's wrong."

She literally growled at me then and I was damned glad she'd left her rifle in the plane.

"Aw, come down off your high horse, lady," I said. "I've got you and you know it. We're all rapists up here, only we use our dicks in different ways. And anyway it's all about finished for all of us. Any year now the Feds will wise up to what they've got here and then they'll grab it away from us to fill their own pork barrel. We might as well get in our licks while we can."

"That's what I despise about you most, Sam," she says after a bit. "You're such a cynic."

Well, we left it at that. We couldn't find the kids that summer so we just waited for them to come out. As they did, toward the end of August. They were brown and bug-bit and calloused and dirty but they'd made it all right. Their summer of dredging and crevassing the creek had produced a little more than four ounces of gold, most of it dust but a few nuggets the size of pinheads and one as big as a pencil eraser. They both looked bigger and certainly wiser. I'm sure they were screwing. Dude wore that silly-ass look of a man who's gotten away with it, and Suzy had that smug quiet air about her that women get when they've learned the score. But she wasn't pregnant anyway.

When Dude pulled the canoe up on the gravel bar and stood there waiting for us, Jack walked up to him, whitefaced, and slugged him in the chops. The kid staggered back but didn't go down. He just stood there grinning. Then the mothers were upon them both, hugging and chirping and kissing the way they will do. And shaking their fists at poor Jack, who'd only done a father's duty.

My punishment of Susan wasn't physical. I merely sent her away to a Catholic girls' boarding school in California for the next two years, and after that to Sarah Lawrence College in Bronxville, New York, for an education among the bull dykes.

Two years later, Dude ran away again. He headed Outside, lied about his age, and joined the army to fight in Vietnam. He became a Ranger and he won a lot of medals but he came home with a head wound. Thereafter, he wore thick glasses. But he was as jolly and headstrong as ever. I always did love that kid.

CHAPTER TWENTY

*T*HE HUNTER'S name was Malec Mummad-Afi but we called him the Big Man from Eye-Ran. He'd been a wheel in the Shah's government (one of the top men in Savak, the Iranian intelligence outfit, according to Jep) and when that regime got the boot from the imams, he made a beeline for the States, where he had plenty of wealthy pals who owed him favors. Not that he needed dough. Like most of them, he'd salted away a few million petrobucks in a Swiss account, and he got out early enough to take most of his nonliquid loot with him: Persian rugs, ancient crockery, finely wrought bronzes, rare rich furs, all of his hunting trophies and his armory. The Big Man was quite a hunter, we were told. He had run four Grand Slams on sheep with the standard calibers— .270, .30/06, .300 H. & H. Magnum, and .308 Winchester— and he was one ram shy of the world's first Grand Slam in .17 Magnum. That's the tiniest bullet built.

Sheep hunters are a fanatical lot. Once a man's got ram fever, nothing else can give him a kick. Not lions or leopards, not Cape buffalo or griz. Not even elephants in heavy cover. They fall in love with the anguish of altitude: long, ankle-busting stalks over bare rock with the wind like a skinning knife down your neck and the air so thin that you inhale it by the molecule. It's not unusual for a sheep addict to walk, run, scramble on hands and knees, or skin along by his fingertips on ledges an inch wide, for a distance of ten or twelve circuitous miles, in order to get a shot at a ram he initially spotted not half a mile from him. And then pass up the shot because the horns weren't right. The Big Man from Eye-Ran was one of these.

Mummad-Afi and his entourage arrived at the lodge by Jet Ranger helicopter from Anchorage on a crisp October afternoon. He was a scimitar-slim, dagger-beaked man in his early sixties with a narrow, steel-blue jaw and hard brown hawk's eyes that rarely blinked, and then only in a slow, camera's shutter manner as if he were taking a time exposure. His entourage consisted of a valet cum bodyguard, his personal shikari, and two high-priced houris, a dark and slinky Latina named Victoria de los Pueblos and a blonde, rather plump Mittel European who went by the nom de boudoir of Svetlana Liberté. The ladies shivered delicately in the icy breeze from the glacier and sniffed with evident disgust as they picked their dainty way along the duckboards that led from the helipad across mudflats to the lodge's walkway. They paid no attention to the mountains soaring around them, gone pale blue at this season with the first frosting of snow.

The valet, a hardbitten limey named Gates, hauled what looked like a ton of luggage to the main guest cabin, while the shikari took charge of the gun cases—fully half a dozen of them, all gold-monogrammed calfskin. The shikari was a leathery old Pathan tribesman from Afghanistan and he immediately fell into the waiting clutches of Charlie Blue. They must have found some Ur language in common, for soon the two were inseparable, chumming together and talking away a mile a minute about God only knows what—killing, no doubt.

"Ah, quite elegant in a homely manner," said Mummad-Afi as he warmed his backside before the huge stone fireplace and sipped a cup of tea. His eyes studied the heads on the wall—the giant palmate horns of moose white in the gloom, the gaping jaws of bears, the silver-ruffed, chocolate-and-ivory spread of caribou, and three splendid Dall sheep, each a full curl and a half of yellow-horned beauty, their snow-white necks arched as if in wariness. "Tell me, Mister Slade, did you shoot them all yourself?"

"No sir," gruffed Jack. "My wife killed the most of them, and a few were left us by grateful clients. I haven't killed an animal except in self-defense in ten years or more."

"Your wife must be quite a sportswoman."

"One of the best shots I've ever been privileged to watch," said Jack.

"And you no longer shoot," continued the Big Man. "A pity. What is it? You have lost your taste for the blood? I am told that many hunters undergo that change later in their careers, though it has not yet overtaken me."

"Not so much that," said Jack, "but more that I know precisely how many animals we can afford to take out of this country every year without depleting the stock or degrading it. And I reserve the harvestable animals for my clients. Oh, we take some culls for meat—a couple of moose a year, a black bear if it's proving troublesome and trying to break in the larder, maybe a caribou or a few blacktail deer, and of course ptarmigan, grouse, ducks and geese in season—but my wife does most of that shooting. I'm too busy around the place, either guiding or doing repairs, to spare the time. My son does some shooting, too."

"Yes, the young war hero. Mister Morgan speaks highly of him. Where is he at the moment?"

"I sent him up to the first spike camp with the packhorses. We'll head up there tomorrow. By the time we get in, Dude should have scouted out the country pretty thoroughly, so we'll know what's at home and where it's hanging out. It's Dall you're after, I take it."

"Yes. I need a ram with at least forty inches of curl to the side to complete my Slam in .17 caliber." He studied the heads on the wall again. "Those all would seem to fill the order. I hope you have more of the same on the premises."

Slade laughed. "The premises? This is big country, Mister

Mummad-Afi. It's no supermarket. I know we have at least a dozen forty-inch rams in my territory, but just where they are and how we're going to collect one is something unpredictable as I'm sure you, as an old sheep hunter, are well aware."

"Of course. I didn't mean to sound condescending."

"Frankly, Mister Mummad-Afi . . ."

"Call me Mike, Mister Slade. All my American friends do."

"Right. What I was about to say, Mike, is I'm a bit leery of this .17-caliber business. You're only throwing a 40-grain bullet and a Dall sheep is a tough customer. A ram of the size we're talking about will weigh two hundred pounds dressed, a good two fifty on the hoof. I'm even uneasy going as light as .270 on them, for fear that you'll hit them clean enough but they'll stagger off and fall over a cliff before you can collect them. Then it's goodbye horns."

"True. But already I have killed Pamir markhor, Tibetan argali, Marco Polo sheep, a hefty Rocky Mountain bighorn and a fair-sized Stone sheep with the small bullet. Not to mention aoudad, bharal and a 175-pound Turkestani urial. None of them exactly sissies. And all of them dead to a single bullet, as I intend to take this final Dall ram."

"Well, there's nothing I hate worse than losing a good animal to inadequate firepower. It's a waste and, in my eyes, a sin against the gods of these mountains."

"Agreed. But the challenge of this Slam is to take all of the major sheep species with one shot from the smallest available caliber, and I am but a single short step from success. If I round out my sheep Slam, I intend to continue by taking one of each member of the subfamily Caprinae, which as you doubtless know includes all the wild sheep and goats on the planet. To that end I would also like to pursue the local representative, *Oreamnos americanus*, or what you call the Rocky Mountain goat, though it is actually, according to some taxonomists, closer to the Antilopinae than the Caprinae, *n'estce pas?*"

"If you say so," said Jack. "Anyway, we've got some good billies in these parts, but again I'm damn nervous about going .17 on them. They're a hell of a lot bigger and tougher than these Dalls, and though their horns are short and brittle they've been known to kill grizzlies and cougars with them. Mean customers. And the country they inhabit is even meaner. A lot of sheep hunters I know would rather go for brown bear or griz than mess with billies, mainly because it's too damn easy to fall off a mountain during the stalk. I've seen the bastards walk straight up a vertical cliff like you or I would mount a curb on a city street."

"I can climb," Mummad-Afi said stiffly. Clearly, he was getting miffed at Jack's putdown of his popgun approach to big-game hunting. I figured I'd better cool them both down.

"Of course you can, Mike," I said, "and Jack knows it. Don't you, Jack-O? Sure. And you can shoot, too, otherwise you wouldn't have taken all those markdowns and argyles and urinals you were mentioning just before, would he Jack, old Buddy? All Jack means is he hopes you realize this won't be any walk-up-to-'em-and-take-your-picnic, right? Right. And you know thatanyway, don't you, Mike, old boy? Now listen, you're not so strict a Believer that you wouldn't be able to handle a little Glenlivet, would you, Mike?"

"Well," says the Big Man, mollified a bit by my gushing, "I guess the Ayatollah isn't watching, is he?" That got us all laughing and Jack started asking him about the revolution of the imams and what was going to happen in that sorry country while I poured us all a good-sized dollop of Scotch and then Josey came in with some gooseliver canapes and we stoked up the fire while Gates, the valet, served us more drinks and before you knew it, everybody was happy and looking forward to tomorrow and the Big Sheep Hunt with the Little Gun.

After dinner—it was a very nice salmon mousse with dill sauce, both the fish and the herbs home grown: Josey was a damn fine cook—Jack went down to the river to check the moorings on the boats and the plane. I went with him.

"Listen," I said, "what are you trying to do? Don't lean on that guy so hard. You'll queer this whole deal."

"What deal?"

"I mean the hunt. Jep's trying to get this guy to invest in the company. He needs more development money and Mummad-Afi's got millions just lying around collecting bank interest. He figures the gun-nut approach is the way to reach him."

"Well, fuck Jep's deal. I don't like this small-caliber crap. You waste game that way, and also people can get hurt. There was a fellow from Vegas down on Admiralty a few years back hunting browns with a .222 and he hit one all right but then they had to go in after it. It was Buddy Prewitt's party and the bear grabbed Buddy and ate his head for an hors d'oeuvre. If Mummad-Afi wanted to go for bear with that pea shooter of his, I wouldn't take him. As it is, I don't like the notion of going for billies that much either."

"Well, he's got to be good if he's collected all he says he has with it."

"His tracker told Charlie that he took two of those Asian sheep from a helicopter, and he shot the desert bighorn down in Mexico from a Land Rover."

"But he hit 'em."

"It's not the same thing. I'm going to keep a close eye on him and back him with the '06 on anything tricky."

Jack tightened up the lines on the jetboat and we walked back up the dock. Through the windows of the big cabin we could see one of the houris walking back and forth. The light was on in the bedroom. I guess it was the other girl's turn and this one didn't want to watch.

"That's another thing," Jack says. "I don't like taking these twists up there with us either. Usually the guys you send me bring women who know the mountains and the woods, or at least can handle it without a lot of pussy stuff. These two look like the farthest they ever walked was to the bidet."

"I'll take care of them, and Gates will be along to help."

"How do you figure that Gates? He's a close-mouthed bastard, looks tough. Did you notice at dinner? He's carrying."

"Probably an ex-merc. There's hundreds of them working for the Arabs these days now that Africa's lost its attraction."

Jack sat on an oil drum at the foot of the dock and I lit a cigar. The moon was just easing up, low over the glacier, and the light was that deep-sea blue it gets, with silver highlights off the boulders and the ice, and the moraines weaving in and out in the glimmer like black snakes.

"We've come some distance, pally, haven't we?" I told him.

"A ways, yeah," he said, nodding. "I'll be sixty next month. An old fart. Kind of hard to believe."

"I just pretend it isn't happening," I told him. "But try to tell that to your pecker."

We laughed and he went back into the lodge. The houri was still walking back and forth in front of the window as I passed on my way to my own cabin. I wondered what would happen if I whistled her out to look at the moon.

CHAPTER TWENTY-ONE

THE WEATHER held fair under a high Arctic sky, the blue dome broken only by a scattering of those pancake-shaped lenticular clouds that look like melting UFOs. The ride to the first camp was a short one, a mere fifteen miles, because Jack believed in easing his clients into the rigors of the hunt and seeing how they responded along the way. Even at that my crotch, after the first five miles, felt like it had split halfway to my bellybutton. Mummad-Afi was a seasoned horseman, though, sitting the saddle as light as a lancer with a rifle tucked in the boot under his right leg and a heavy handgun on his hip. He was dressed in dark brown whipcord and knee-high riding boots with a flat-brimmed black vaquero's hat on his head, and you could have taken him for a grandee the way he rode. Surprisingly, the houris too were good riders, though they complained to one another anyway in high nasal voices, just to keep their tongues in shape, I figured. As we climbed away from the river, you could see the glacier sprawling below, and beyond it the ragged rise of the Dead Mounties.

Gates had been hanging back with the Pathan and Charlie

Blue who were leading the four pack horses, but now he trotted up and reined into step with me. He sat his horse heavily but with no concern, not a practiced rider but reasonably at home with it.

"How did the range get its name, Mister Healey?"

"Back during the war," I told him. "There was a party of Japanese Imperial Marines on the prowl in here, interdicting the Alaska Highway where it came up through the Yukon and veered west into Alaska. They were running raids on the work camps, blowing culverts and such. The Canucks sent a patrol of Mounties in to ferret them out but the Japs laid an ambush, killed the lot."

"Fascinating," says Gates, his eyes glittering. He had a big beefy face starred with old acne scars and square, hard-looking hands with nicks on his knuckles. Some valet. "What happened to the Japanese?"

"Probably died off finally, with the weather and all. They never found them. Charlie Blue, the old Indian back there, says he met them a few times during his travels in the mountains, but you can't believe what he says. Half the time he lives in his head, back in the tribal past. At any rate, they haven't made trouble for anyone since the mid-1950s, when they apparently scragged a party of molybdenum prospectors who were working the country."

"Maybe we'll run across them," he says with more avidity than I felt.

"You're more than just a gentleman's gentleman, aren't you, Gates? I get the feeling you've been around."

"Here and there," he says. "Malaya. The Congo. Rhodesia and Namibia. In those days you took what you could get. There wasn't much money in it. None of those governments could pay the way the Arabs and the Persians can. We did it more for love than anything else."

"I don't care much for the rough stuff anymore," I said. "Back when I was a young punk I helled around some, but now I'm too slow. Old Mike, though, he looks like a pretty tough cookie."

"He's very good, yes. Especially with the rifle. But his hands have hardened up on him. He can't do this anymore."

Gates made a flicking motion with his right hand, toward

the pommel of his saddle, and sudden as a conjurer he had a squat blue revolver in it. Pointed dead on my Adam's apple. He spun it in a blue blur and it was gone.

"Took care of gentlemen, did you?"

"Yes," he said with a sudden, brilliant smile. "Rewarding work that, taking care of gentlemen."

We stopped for lunch in a high saddle where a spring bubbled out of the rocks and a flat boulder served us as a table. Josey had packed a lunch of cold partridge, smoked salmon and potato salad. A cooler of beer and white wine accompanied these goodies, though the two houris preferred a puff on their hookah followed by iced tea. The ganja loosened them up some and they actually chatted with us heathen feringis, commenting for the first time on the scenery.

"Is a bleak black cawntry this," said Victoria de los Pueblos. "Cold. Brrr."

"This is a nice warm day, lady," said Strang, the other wrangler. "You put a couple clouds over that sun and you'll feel what it can be like, even in midsummer. I've seen it snow in July here."

"Like Dagestan and the Pamir," said Svetlana Liberté. "I thought I had cut myself loose from all that. But Mickey, he like the wild places."

"Why didn't you two stay back at the lodge?" Strang asked. "You'd have been a lot more comfortable there."

"Mickey need us," says Victoria. "Only we two can read his fortune for him. One alone cannot do it. Not with Mickey."

Strang cast an admiring look at the Persian. He shook his head.

"Waaaal," he drawled in his best Texican accent, "Ah shore wouldn't mind a little look-see under the skirts of the future. Anytime you two gypsy ladies want to moonlight a bit, jest keep me in mind." He hitched at his crotch and winked broadly. The ladies giggled. Mummad-Afi snapped something in a gobbledygook lingo and they sobered up quick, gathered their gear together and moved over to a rock near where the horses were picketed.

"What are those small creatures out there in the rocks, Jack?" asked Mummad. "Marmots?"

"Yep."

"I would like to see if the sights on the .17 are still in alignment. Would it disturb our hunting plans if I took a few shots?"

"We're far enough away from where we'll be hunting that it won't be a problem," Jack says. Mummad-Afi snapped his fingers and Gates brought the rifle from the saddle boot. It was a Weatherby Mark V, custom modified for the .17 Magnum round, with a stock in Circassian walnut and the receiver and trigger guard chased in gold. The fore end was knurled, Mannlicher fashion, and Mike pointed out the carving to us with pride: a flattened tiger, about to spring, the knurl its broad, evil-eyed head. The tail sinuated down and wound tensely around the floor plate. You almost expected to see it twitch. The rifle had a set trigger plated in gold, as was the hair trigger forward of it.

"A beautiful weapon," says Jack.

"It shoots even more beautifully," Mummad replied. He wound the sling tightly on his forearm and took an elbow rest on his knees. The rifle cracked and three hundred yards down the slope a marmot exploded in gouts of red meat. The others dove for their holes but Mummad worked the bolt swiftly and nailed another as it was about to disappear. That shot was even longer. He could shoot all right.

"Would you like to take a poke?" he says to Jack, proffering the rifle.

"No. I kind of like those little guys, and anyway I don't think they'll be showing their heads for a bit."

Mummad shrugged and looked back down the slope. A pair of ravens, attracted by the gunfire, appeared in the distance and swept rapidly in when they spotted the marmot bodies. With a lightning movement, Mummad raised the rifle to his shoulder and blasted a raven out of the air. As it fell limp and twisting in a cloud of feathers, he worked the bolt and sighted in on the second. Jack sprang forward and knocked the rifle barrel upward.

"Dammit, no!" he said hoarsely. "You don't shoot ravens."

Mummad looked around, his hawk's eyes black with rage. His jaw tightened as he stood up.

"Never lay hands on my weapon," he said in a kind of hiss. Then he regained control of himself and relaxed his shoulders. He smiled icily. "What is that? Why not shoot ravens? They are carrion eaters, filthy birds, robbers of nests and eaters of the young."

"We don't shoot them," Jack said. "In this country they're gods. Even a starving man would think long and hard before he'd kill a raven, and if he did, it would go down hard."

Mummad laughed. "Gods," he said. "Heathen nonsense, I say, though if you feel strongly about it of course I shall shoot no more."

When Jack had slapped at the rifle, I saw Gates's hand go to his waistband. So that was where he carried the piece, forward on the left side. A good item to remember.

Charlie Blue was upset. He stood there, wrinkled and disheveled as always, but with a dreadful woebegone look on his flat face. He kept shaking his head from side to side and muttering under his breath. The Pathan, whose name was Sayed, asked him something in their muckaluck lingo and Charlie pointed to the sky. There were tears in his old eyes. The Pathan nodded, as if in agreement. The old gods live, all right, at least back in the drear mountains wherever they stand.

We got to camp before dark. Dude rode out to meet us with a thermos of hot coffee, a flask of brandy and bad news.

"There were four nice rams up in the col where we nailed that big one two years ago," he told Jack. "Good rams, curl and a half and then some. All by themselves. Hadn't joined up with the ewes yet. That was day before yesterday and I kept close watch on them till dark. This morning when I went back up there they had split. I followed their sign across the col and down the far side into that little valley where the waterfall comes in from the east, and they were feeding along slow and easy-like. Then something spooked them and they made tracks to the north."

"What did you see?"

"I thought maybe it was griz. The horses were acting funny that night. But I couldn't find any sign."

"Men?" (Gates had come up to listen and now his eyes lit

up again the way they had when I told him about the Japs.)

"No smoke. No horseshit that I could spot. No tracks. But they could have been afoot. That's all hard rock down there. You know the place. Maybe Charlie could see something that I missed."

"No. We'll have a look in the morning, but they probably just spooked for the hell of it. The rut's coming on fast now and they get twitchy."

"I was going to head back down to the lodge in the morning with Strang and two of the ponies," Dude said after a bit. "Maybe we'd better stay. With those sheep gone you may have to work up to number two in a couple of days. And you could use the extra eyes."

"We'll see in the morning."

I walked over to where Charlie and the Pathan were standing beside their horses. Charlie looked sadder than ever. I put my arm around him and tried not to smell the stink of him: stale grease and woodsmoke and an old man's coppery sweat.

"What's the matter, Shaman?" I asked him. "You still fretting about Raven?"

"You damn right, Sammy. That was a dumb move." He shook his wattles. "And now the sheep are gone. Let's hope that's the worst of it. Something bad comes of this, you damn right it does. Even this old Indian here," and he pointed to the Pathan, "feels it coming. Look out there." His eyes went west. A few skinny tendrils of cirrus were weaving up over the horizon, blood red in the last light. "Weather on the way. Snow. You smell it?"

"All I can smell is you, Charlie."

"You're no goddam lilac bush yourself, Sammy."

"Too much horseback," I said. "It pounds all the farts out my pores."

But he was right. There was weather on the way, snow probably at this time of year. But that would work as much in our favor, provided it wasn't a blizzard, as it would against us. Though it would make the sheep, with their white hides, harder to spot against the hills we'd be glassing, it would show us which way they were moving when we found their trail.

We headed down into camp—a low log cabin set in against

the cliffs, its roof built of slate from the rockfalls, a thin blue ribbon of smoke coiling up from the stovepipe and then flattening when it hit the cold air that was moving in ahead of the front from the west.

Long after midnight, as is the aging man's prerogative, I slipped out the door of the cabin to take a pee. Norman Ormandy says that there's nothing sadder than an old fag who can't get it up anymore. I say there's nothing sadder than a sixty-year-old former bush pilot turned pimp and oil promoter who lusts for young ladies and yet can only get a hard-on thanks to his weakened kidneys. A piss hard-on, that's what we call it. The kind you fuck your hand with. Can't let it go to waste, you know. Not a rarity like that.

And I was the guy who fought it out on the dock, with that strange light turning everything to hard-edged death, the moss-grown logs, the splinters crackling underfoot, those faces glaring bone-white, hollow-eyed, mouths full of dark vapors going silver in the glare, like salmon rolling when you snag them in the riffles—illegally, of course—or the inside of a bear's mouth when he comes for you through the prickles and a ray of weak sunlight stabs him in the tonsils, and all the while— God, how great that night was!—I'm moving and shifting and up on my toes, not even feeling the bones break in my hand on Gainey's ugly pan, no, not quite: feeling them crack and feeling the first deadened sting of it up to my shoulder but then the pain itself lighting a spark in my eyes that feeds like a firetongue on his black blood, races, roars, not caring now about the Colt in the crab pot, knowing I can take this fat cuckold and prove to these apes I'm king of the cannery town— what a crown, what a realm!—but if I don't kill his raggedy ass I may as well haul tail back to Illinois and peddle shoes again: no: never that no more no more: stunted towns and stinking culverts and the big thrill of the year when they plug Tuohy coming down the El staircase, weak old bandit: but then when I've suckered Gainey the way I want him, young as I was then, tough, knowing how to use the weight, and I have him set up, confident with his slow swing to my ribs that he can take me out with one punch, and I open him up like a can of peaches and set and deliver: the reward of that well-thrown fist gathering interest in a bank long gone bust: and then he merely staggers. Well. That was the frigging end of me all right.

And now.

An old man pissing in the snow.

Yes, as Charlie predicted, it was snowing now, slow flakes, no wind behind them, a good tracking snow. In the morning, they would go out after sheep and I would lie like a goat waiting to try my shot at the houris. All Jep wanted was for the hunt to go smoothly. Nothing I could add to that aspect that I hadn't already. Jack was working good, and Dude was going to stay.

If we could get Mummad's money, we could develop the glacier oil, and we'd be set for keeps then. We'd find Jack a new place, better than this one: maybe down in New Zealand, or Hawaii, New Guinea might suit him better. Up in the Owen-Stanleys, there were still practicing headhunters.

And if Gates should kill Jack over some slight to his boss . . . That man was primed for it all right, ready to go. . . But no, not Jack. Not all those years—India, China, the Dakota.

Why not?

He's not your brother, is he?

Ellie says family first, pals last. Fuck it. If Gates . . .

Then I heard the moan, and the old in-out in the snow. I moved around the edge of the cabin to the corral and they were at it in the lee corner, Strang and the Victory of the People, over a hay bale Dude had hurled up, with the horses uneasy around them—charged up, do you reckon?—and Strang's jeans down over his scrawny ass and her one naked leg up and kicking as if to bruise the snow: it was Strang groaning as he plugged her with her chittering away chipmunk-like in Spanish and wriggling under him: damn, I'm sorry I lost that piss hard-on, but wait, what's this coming on? Something Ellie never gave me.

"What do you suggest, Mister Healey?"

The voice over my shoulder limped me out for keeps that night. Gates, of course. And he had the pistol in his hand.

"Uh."

"By rights I should shoot the both of them," he whispered, "but it would only ruin the hunting trip, wouldn't it? And my employer values his sport in many ways indecipherable to us plebeians. He prefers the ram to the ewe. Anyway he's got another one warm in the sack with him right now. No harm done."

He took me by the arm and led me back into the cabin.

CHAPTER TWENTY-TWO

*A*LL *THE* next day it snowed, a gray veil that obscured the far peaks and cut visibility to a quarter of a mile. They went out anyway. Jack, Gates and Mummad hunted up toward the north. Dude and Strang went west. Charlie and Sayed checked the col where Dude had glassed the four rams earlier, found nothing, and then headed east into a broken country of ridges and rotten lava. I stayed in camp with the houris but they responded indifferently to my suggestion that we while away the hours by playing "Doctor" so I ended up splitting firewood, brewing coffee and organizing a suppertime stew of caribou bits, carrots and onions. Svetlana knitted; Victoria played double solitaire.

"Nothing," said Jack when they came in, sodden with wet snow, on toward dark.

"Snowflakes, slippery rock and a covey of ptarmigan," reported Dude.

"A bear dug out two marmots and ate them but missed a third; the mate of that dead raven hunched in a snag near open water; and this," said Charlie Blue. He tossed an empty cartridge case on the table. Jack picked it up and read the base.

"Seven point seven millimeter," he said. "Probably from a type 99 rifle. The Japs used them in the Aleutians during the war."

"I told you they were still around," said Charlie.

"Unlikely," says Jack. "I've seen plenty of Indians and Aleuts carrying old Japanese rifles, and anyway that brass is pretty well corroded. It could have been lying around since the days of the Mounties. But we'll keep watch tonight and tomorrow we'll pull out and head on down to the lodge. I'm sorry, Mister Mummad, but it looks like a washout."

"Nonsense," Mike answers. "I'm not concerned with Japanese stragglers. We are heavily armed, better armed than they, and they must be old men by now."

"The weather is not going to get any better," says Jack, "and those sheep have cleared out of here. To move up to the higher camps with this snow would take more feed for the horses than we have with us, and the only meat we could kill for ourselves is down in the valleys by now. We'd have supply problems."

"Call in some supplies," Mummad says. "Send your son or Strang or both of them down to the lodge tomorrow. They can fly food in for us. I want my ram, and that is that."

"Don't worry about watches," said Gates. "I'll stay up all night. I'm used to it."

Dude broke out his fiddle and, grinning, began to saw away:

> Oh I been sheep hunting all my life
> And all I got is my Barlow knife.
> Barlow handle and Barlow blade,
> Best damn knife that ever was made.

The next day we moved up to the second camp, hunted the snow for two days more, found nothing, no sign even, and then moved up into the really rough country to the northeast where steep valleys could provide browse and pasturage for wild goats and sheep. There were moose in the brakes along the valley creeks, cows and yearling calves, one of which we killed for meat, and signs of bear moving nervously, feeding themselves up for the long winter sleep. But no sheep.

And no Japanese.

Charlie and the Pathan scouted for human sign every day, leaving the sheep tracking to Jack and Dude. They found nothing.

On the fifth day, with the ladies nervous and bushwhacky with the cold and the lack of action, and with Gates surly at the lack of human targets, they found rams. Three good rams and one for the record books.

Mummad stalked and shot it on a high cliff face with the sun hot on the gray rock and rivulets of snow melt staining the cliff black in long broken tracks, and the sheep staggered to the hit, then pulled itself together and bounded over the spine of the ridge. They followed and we watched them, Gates through binoculars and I with the 20x spotting scope, half a mile away on another ridge.

The sheep wandered weakly out onto a long point of rock that fell away to either side a thousand feet into whitewater gulches. Then it lay down, boxing its legs catlike under itself. Its big yellow-horned head swayed like a wooly pendulum to the sickness of its wound. We could see Jack and Mummad talking where they lay against boulders at the beginning of the point. Finally, Jack got up and walked out toward the sheep.

When he got to it, the ram rose—suddenly, powerfully, as if it had merely been taking a nap—and, trapped, it slammed forward into Slade's belly, bending and then bucking him out and over the edge of the point. He managed to snag the lip of the rock with his fingertips.

The sheep began to dance around his hands, as if it were purposely trying to stomp his fingers.

All this while, Mummad stood watching, his rifle slung over his right shoulder. We could hear Jack shouting to him but he seemed not to hear. He wanted this to be a one-shot kill, and he was waiting for the ram to die.

Then Dude appeared behind the Persian, took in the scene in one glance, cuffed Mummad on the ear and ran out onto the point with a revolver in his hand. The sheep spun away from Jack's clutching hands and started toward Dude. Dude raised the revolver and we saw it kick and then heard the report as the sheep sprawled face-first down onto the edge of the point, then skidded slowly over the edge. Only as it fell did Mummad seem to recover his senses. He raised both arms pleadingly and lurched forward as if to stop the sheep in its accelerating skid. But then the ram was gone.

We saw it slide loose of the adhesion of the rock, then tumble backward into open air, turning and spinning as it fell, its yellow horns winking alternately in shade and sunlight until it crashed finally on the dark boulders far below. Its horns were shattered to raw red stubs.

We saw Jack walk stiffly up to where Mummad stood, shoulders slumped as he stared down into the abyss. Jack grabbled the rifle from Mummad's hands and smashed the stock against a boulder, smashed it to splinters of walnut and glass and just the scarred barrel left in his hands. Then he grabbed Mummad by the front of his jacket and went to work on his patrician Persian pan.

"Bloody 'ell!" hollered Gates. "I've got to get over there!"

"Take it easy, pal," I told him. "He won't kill your boss. He's just teaching him a lesson in priorities."

Where his face wasn't blue-green with bruises, Mummad was white with fury. He stormed into Jep's office in Juneau three days later with me trailing behind and trying to cool him down.

"I want Slade ruined," he yipped at Jep. "Dead, if possible. You say there is oil on his land. I want it. And you will arrange it. And Slade and his son and his wife will leave that country, forever, and without a penny."

"Now wait a minute, Mike . . ."

"No minutes, no seconds, nothing. It will be done. If it is not, there are things your attorney general has an interest in. You know as well as I to which matters I refer."

Gates stood behind him, arms folded across his chest, one hand dangling not far from the butt of the pistol where it snugged against his cushioned belly.

Things moved swiftly. Jep called in his lawyers and before the year was out the President of the United States had pleased the environmentalists once more by declaring yet another hefty chunk of Alaska a National Monument—this one the Blue Bear National Monument, sole remaining stomping grounds of that shy and reclusive creature already on the Endangered Species

List. Compared with vast and far more spectacular acreage he had thus removed from the clutches of hunters, anglers and loggers back in 1978, this was a small bite and little outcry arose from the gun fraternity or the exploiters. The national need for oil, however, allowed him to exempt petroleum developers from access to the Monument. Since Morgan Petro was most familiar with drilling procedures in that latitude, the lease went to Jep's boys, with development funding courtesy of M-A Mineralogy Ltd. of Geneva and Palm Beach, Malec Mummad-Afi, president and chairman of the board.

"Why couldn't you stop them?"

"Look," I told him, "I only work there. Anyway, it was the Feds who made the decision, not Jep or the rest of them."

"Bullshit! Don't give me that crapola. You know as well as I do that it was the Big Man from Eye-Ran who called the shot. And Jep went along with him."

"You know that Jep loves you like a goddam brother, why get on him?"

"When Jep sees big bucks, he goes for them, the way Mummad goes for big rams only with a larger caliber load. How the hell did you know there was developable oil on the property?"

"A lucky guess."

He stared at me out of that warped, scarred face, his eyes at angles to each other.

"You lying cocksucker," he said, way deep and grating like he did. "I saw the holes where your doodlebugs were shooting. Dude found them four years ago. I figured you'd struck out and that's why you weren't in here already, drilling. But just to prevent you, I changed the registration on the homestead. You don't have your half say anymore, Sam. But a hell of a lot of good that does me, with the Feds in on it now."

"I don't know what you're talking about," I said. "Anyway the government wants oil for the folks, and they want the glacier for the posey-fuckers, and that's that. It's done, Jack-O. Over. Finished for keeps. You're out."

"Unless the appeals work."

"I don't have to tell you."

He got up and walked over to the gun cabinet. Then he

looked around the big room of the lodge, at all the heads and hides, the books and paintings, and at the furniture he'd built over the years. There was a big fire roaring in the stand-up fireplace, and outside the wind was howling down from the Circle with a snow-filled vengeance.

"You're pounding sand down a legal rathole," I told him. "Give it up. Jep will set you up in another place, wherever you want, here in Alaska or over in the Yukon—you always loved that country in the Ogilvies, where the new highway is open now, the Dempster—or even overseas if you want. There's still good country in the Owen-Stanley Range, in New Guinea there."

He took down a rifle—that .22-250 of his that he was so proud of—clean kills at seven hundred yards, even in a cross-wind—he was no better than Mummad in that respect. He worked the bolt and then pulled it, checked the lands for fouling, took down a cleaning rod and ran a dry patch through it. He loved those pieces, always played around with them, the way a man whittled in the old days.

"No," he said at last. "This country is my whole life, the only part of it that counts. I'm sixty years old and I'm not going to learn a new country even if I wanted to try it. I'm not going."

"What can you do?" I asked him.

"Let them try to come in here," he said. "Josey and Dude and I, we'll make it a tough road in." He reassembled the action on the rifle and socked the bolt home. "And if that doesn't work, I can teach them a little lesson my father once taught me."

The light was going fast now and I had to fly back down to Gurry Bay and then catch the Alaska Airlines jet from there down to Ske-daddle. More stuff with the lawyers.

"You don't hold anything against me, do you pally?" I said.

"You'll be the last one to die," he said.

And he wasn't kidding.

PART THREE

THE GLACIER

1981

CHAPTER TWENTY-THREE

SOMETHING IS moving out there, something so furtive that even the dogs cannot hear it. Stealthier than the cold wind falling from the glacier down through the tops of the pines. Quieter than the slow swirl of ice water over the rocks of the eddies. No wolf ever prowled so carefully, nor any weasel. Maybe it's all in my mind, she thought. But I'd better.

Josey Slade slipped out of bed as quietly as possible to avoid waking her husband and pulled on her sealskin mukluks. The room was cold. Her breath puffed pale in the halfdark before dawn and she dressed quickly, catching a glimpse of herself in the dressing table mirror as she writhed into her longjohns. Funny, she thought, the face and hands of an old woman on the body of a girl. We age from the extremities inward. And it's only the outer parts the rest of the world sees. More than half a century old and I still don't need a bra. I guess that's something.

She took the pistol from the night table and went into the main hall. From the dark walls, fierce or benign according to species, stared the bright eyes of animals: moose, caribou,

Dall or Stone sheep; bears black and brown and blue and grizzled, some of them peering sideways around shelves freighted with books. Lynxes, their ears bristling, snarled in silence at a Gauguin nude across the hall, or glowered with yellow glass eyes down a Provençal road by Cézanne. The dead eyes of the trophies had a deep detachment, the seeming wisdom of gurus, she thought. She had mentioned it once to her son Dude when he was home from the war, recovering from his wound, and he had laughed. "Everything dead looks wiser than life," he said. "Don't let them kid you."

A coal snapped in the huge stone fireplace behind her but she did not flinch. The sound she was seeking had come from the outside. She opened the front door and slid out into the shadows under the weather-bleached moose rack overhead. On either side of the door, pegs had been set in the spruce logs for the convenient hanging of flyrods, waders, hip boots, firearms, saws, axes—the daily tools of their trade—and from the porch a path led down to the river, ending at a pier where the boats and the plane were moored. She heard the rhythmic rocking of the plane's floats on the river. The light was dark blue out there and snakes of fog curled on the current. She walked quietly down the path, between stands of shoulder-high Arctic cotton that gleamed pearlwhite in the gloom. The pistol was ready in her hand. But there was nothing. No one. She checked the mud carefully for fresh sign, but in that light she could not be sure. She tested the lines on the boats and the plane and they were secure. Far out in the dark a spawning salmon rolled, a heavy shivering sound. Just my imagination, she thought. Just a bad dream. And she went back to the lodge.

So many bad dreams lately, she thought as she brewed a pot of tea in her kitchen.

And why not? The Outside is coming closer every day. We've lost the place but Jack won't admit it. He wants to fight. And we can't win, and he knows it. She looked around the kitchen at her handiwork—the time-darkened breadbaskets she had woven over the years from river reeds, her pots and pans fire-scarred from thousands of meals cooked over the ancient wood stove, utensils hanging from the heavy ceiling beams, all catching the light in familiar winking patterns. She could move in the kitchen in the dark, cook a six-course meal in it blindfolded. That had to count for something. Now they say, Get. Do it all over again, someplace else. Of course she had nightmares.

But where else is there for people our age? Africa is finished for the white man. My Spanish is too rusty for repair and my Portuguese nonexistent, so that leaves South America out. Europe maybe—Spain or Ireland, good bird shooting, salmon beats—but Jack has no use for that continent: worse than the Lower Forty-eight, he says. Pussies. New Guinea? Fruit bats and tamed-down headhunters. No chance. Besides, too hot.

The Rocky Mountains—Alberta or Montana perhaps. But Canada is too tame. Even in places like Dawson City and White-horse you feel you're among steers rather than bulls. And Montana is filling up with Californians, or else with writers and movie actors who play at being tough. What is it Dude says? They mainline TV. The only thing on television is sassy Negroes and cutesy he-shes and assholes so stupid they think they are Real People. And soaps. Those women on the bus that time in Seattle. For five stop-and-go miles they had swapped the most horrific gossip. Marlene had to have an abortion because Aggie's husband Storm had raped her and Mark's father had run the business into the ground so he and Jennifer had to sell the house to pay for Duane's sex-change operation. It wasn't till the end, when one of the women mentioned in a bored voice that her own son had the measles, and I knew they were discussing a television program. It was more real to them than their own lives. The worst thing about the Outside was that everything happened Inside.

And if we stay in Alaska, what then, and where? Anchorage has become a northern suburb of Seattle and Fairbanks is little better. Since the Native Claims Settlement Act there is no open land to speak of left for white Alaskans—here, in a state as big as an entire third of the Lower Forty-eight. Land-poor in the vastness. But I suppose we'll have to put up with it. Jack is fighting mad now, but he'll learn to live with it when the fight is over. We have the best things anyway: us. That they can't rip off.

She poured another cup of tea and, on a whim, spiked it with two glugs from a bottle of Courvoisier, then went out on the dock. The morning was coming on and she watched the big black shapes of the king salmon moving up through the current. Just downstream from the dock a hen was digging her redd, scooping the boulders with her dark tail and flipping them clear of the long, tear-shaped oval of gravel in which she would deposit her eggs. Two males circled in the sand-fogged current, watching her. From time to time the larger male drove toward the smaller, his deeply hooked jaw slashing to force the smaller competitor away. Then as the redd neared completion he moved in on the female, darting around her and rolling in the water so his silver belly flashed like a stained mirror. She took position at the upstream end of the redd and lay above the gravel, watching his flashing dance, quivering as her time neared. Then with a climactic shudder she spurted a gout of orange roe into the water and on the instant the male convulsed, a cloudy gusher of semen rushing out and down to follow the eggs to the river bed. It was as if the male's seed were sentient—tendrils of sperm dove after in-dividual egg clusters, encircling them and coating them as they fell whirling in the current to lodge on the gravel. The fertilized eggs would sink deep into the gravel bed and ripen there, emerging next spring as tiny alevins with bits of yolk still at-tached. That would be a time of slaughter. All the trout in the river would be on hand to feast on the salmon fry. Even now they were here, waiting to slash in and gobble eggs as they fell toward the redd. It was just as well, she thought. With the oil operation due for completion next summer, these waters would no longer provide a breeding ground for salmon, or a feeding ground for trout.

The spawned-out hen hovered over her redd, exhausted and slowly dying before Josey's eyes. Instant senescence. From the moment the salmon entered the fresh water to spawn, they began to die. Their hard silver bodies softened and darkened, their jaws warped into hooked stubs, tatters of skin trailed from their bellies and sides. After those final reproductive con-vulsions—I wonder how it feels? Is it a real orgasm? I hope so—the salmon, male and female alike, weakened rapidly and wandered at the will of the current, rolling back down through rapids they had leaped on their way upriver, preyed upon by wolves and bears, eagles and ravens. This hen, the one she was watching, was already badly tattered, her sides and tail frayed with age and dying. Down in Florida, the drugstores display only the boxes that contain bottles of Oil of Olay. Too many old ladies on social security shoplift the magical fluid of youthful skin care. Bring the empty box to the counter and pay for it and you get the bottle. How sad.

She looked again at her own hands. Tough, brown, calloused, starred and crosshatched with the scars of slippery knives and unseen briars. The stump of her right-hand little finger glossy in the morning light. She had been splitting wood one winter morning fifteen years ago and thanks to the cold was not aware she had chopped it off until she saw the dog, Ulf, lapping blood from the snow. She found the finger beside the chopping block and rushed inside with it. Jack was upcountry with a hunting party. She stitched the finger back onto the stub with heavy sewing thread, trying to attach the blood vessels but certain she was doing it improperly. For a while the finger pinked up, but three weeks later it went green and then black. She cut the threads and pulled it off, then threw it into the stove. Oh well, they're good strong hands anyway and they do the work they're meant to do. All the Oil of Olay in the world couldn't help them now, so at least I have that to be thankful for: I'll never be tempted to shoplift for vanity's sake.

Jack came out of the door, buck naked except for moccasins and a towel over his shoulder. His body, too, was still young but surrounded by the badges of age: that scarred face, those crooked hands and big feet splayed and toughened by thousands of miles crossing rough country. Look how his cock flops from side to side when he walks, she thought. Pretty well hung for a mean old fart. She grabbed for his groin as he went by but he spun away with a whoop, snapped at her with the towel, then kicked off his moccasins and dove into the river, taking care to splash her thoroughly with the dive.

"Come on, you dirty old lady," he yelled. "Try that in here where I can fight back."

She stripped and followed him into the icy water, and again they made love as they had the first time, so long ago, among the dying salmon.

"I've got to go down to Gurry Bay this afternoon," he said later as they lay on the dock in the sun. "That fishing party from Portland is due in about three."

"I'll go," she said. "I've got a lot of shopping to do, and you always get so pissed off when you go into town."

"I can't stand to see what they're doing to it. They've got that frigging motel going up for the oil execs and Norman Ormandy is turning the Blue Bear into a goddam pansy garden."

"We're going to have to learn to live with stuff like that," she said.

"I'm damned if I ever will."

"You will."

He ran his fingers over her belly, touching the faded stretch marks from when she had carried Dude. Then he took her maimed hand and held it, rubbing his thumb over the smooth end of the axe-amputated finger stub.

"We've been through a lot of shit together," he said. "We can read it all over each other, like on a goddam map."

After lunch she gassed up the plane, rechecked her shopping list and climbed into the cockpit. Jack held the mooring lines while she ran her takeoff checklist. Then he cast her off and she drifted out into the current, letting the float rudders take her out into the middle. She started the engine and warmed up, then turned downstream to the west into the slight breeze of early afternoon. The sun glared bright on the rolling water and she remembered she'd forgotten her sunglasses. Well, it would only be for a little while, during takeoff. She gunned the motor and raced with the current. The glare flashed in sudden sparkles on her squinting eyes. She felt herself reach takeoff speed, checked the gauge, popped a float clear and pulled back on the stick.

Below her the forest flashed past, dark green and dimming as she climbed, and the glare from the river receded. The engine roared louder for a moment and then there came a sudden blaze of light, brighter than the sun, blinding her. . . .

CHAPTER TWENTY-FOUR

*A*NY TIME now, he thought. Outside the snow was still falling, fat flakes, slow and thick, and the thermometer beyond the windowpane read an even zero. Warm weather for the run. The blue Arctic light was fading fast and he had expected them before dark, but the sound of their snowmobiles would alert him anyway. They had to come today: it was the deadline.

Snowshoes, pack and weaponry stood ready at the back door of the lodge, where the tunnel he had dug through the snowdrifts led out to the cover of spruces on the low ridge to the north. If it got any warmer the tunnel could conceivably collapse, particularly if there were explosions. The snowshoes were short, heavy-framed bearpaws and he knew that their design would cost him speed in the open, but he planned to make his run through rough country—most of it, at least. The pack weighed nearly a hundred pounds, yet he had carried that much or more at a run over this same country often enough to be sure of himself. Most of the weight was high explosives: one-pound bricks of C-4 plastique, off-white in color and as malleable as Silly Putty. Atop the bricks he had packed a hundred yards of det cord, innocuous looking fuzzy stuff that re-sembled loose-braided clothesline. In a side pocket of the pack nestled a box of blasting caps, each the size of a cigarette and covered with aluminum foil. The exploder he carried in his parka pocket, along with the coil of insulated wire.

Boxes of ammo filled most of the top of the pack, shotgun shells and rifle shells and canisters for the stubby M-79 grenade launcher his son had brought back from Southeast Asia. The M-79 was accurate to one hundred fifty yards for precision work, up to three hundred for area fire. Its 40-mm. cartridges were loaded with coils of springy wire, notched every quarter inch so that when the charge detonated they flew into thousands of tiny whirring sawblades. In addition to the grenade launcher, he would carry his Ruger .22-250 rifle mounted with a three-to-nine-power Tasco scope, and loaded with the 55-grain hollow point bullets. The bullets were of the Federal brand, which he thought appropriate. With these, he could hit accurately out to five hundred yards, farther in good light and wind con-ditions. For close work, he had set aside a 12-gauge Remington pump gun along with boxes of both bird- and buckshot. He had spent a long afternoon cutting the pump gun's stock down to the pistol grip and shortening its barrel to a finely filed twenty inches.

The rest of the pack was stuffed with necessities for living on the run: moose jerky, tea, knives, a cup, a match safe, extra sulfur-tip matches, lengths of babiche and a sewing kit to mend his snowshoes if need be, codeine pills, a hand mirror, a light short-handled Hudson Bay cruising ax, a meat saw, a can of WD-40, a can of 3-in-One Oil, an oil rag, a pocket compass (Girl Scout—ironically the most reliable), a surgeon's scalpel and retractor, a packet of number three surgeon's curved silk needles, a bottle of iodine, a box of sterile gauze and another of surgical tape, a needle-nose pliers, a small claw hammer in whose metal handle was nestled a series of ever tinier screwdrivers, and a box of dried apricots (for dessert).

A hell of a load in more ways than one, but he might need every item in it before this business was done.

He went over to pitch a few chunks into the barrel stove and on the way caught a glimpse of himself in the fluted, gold-framed mirror that Josey had found in a Seattle antique shop. The glimpse made him start. Christ, he thought, I scared myself. The face that looked back at him in the deepening dark was lined and deeply scarred, one eye drooping at the outside corner under a flap of shiny scar tissue, the beard bushy and shot through with streaks of white and carcajou yellow but still, at the age of sixty-one, basically black. He was a short, thick-set man with heavy shoulders and a flat belly who moved more like some wild predator than a human being.

I wonder how she loved me after that?

Ugly son of a bitch, you.

He saw again the burst of orange flame above the river, streaked with oily black as it ballooned, and the wing fluttering up and then downward, above the spruces, awkward, clumsy, to splash in the Alugiak. Meant for me, he said to himself for the millionth time.

And she took it.

The radio crackled with static but no voice came through. It had been silent since the previous afternoon when Dude radioed from Juneau that the last appeal had failed. The Feds and Healey had won, as he knew they would. "Get out now, Dad," the boy had said—boy, hell, he was thirty now, wasn't he? "You can't beat 'em. There's other places we can go."

"But not *my* country," he said. "You do as we arranged before you left, kid. You know where."

A long crackling silence, then the key triggered again.

"If you get there." Cut, click.

"I'll be there. Out."

Let the eavesdroppers figure it. The rendezvous could be anywhere back in the Dead Mounties. Sure, they'd have air up watching for him on the passes, but with this late winter weather, the chinook beginning to blow, they would have a hard time following him. He doubted they'd use gunships.

He sat at the smooth-worn table he'd carved himself so many years ago and spread the geo map under the lamp. From the darkness the glass eyes of animals stared down on him off the walls, horns and teeth gleaming cool and ectoplasmic from the gloom. They'd expect him to stay to the passes, making through the range toward the Canadian line—how far? maybe two hundred miles. He would lead them that way, then take to the peaks when they were convinced and double back to the rendezvous.

The construction road, which he had marked in red pencil on the chart, stopped ten miles short of the lodge. He had scouted it all that fall and into the winter. Most of the heavy equipment was parked on a plateau just above the rapids, sumps and tanks drained for the freezeup. He had cached plenty of diesel, though, along with some gasoline.

Better eat now, he told himself. It may be some time before your next hot meal.

He was dozing in the dark by the window when he heard the first snarl of snow machines, and he woke with a snap. Goddammit, old man, what's the matter with you? Snoozing at a time like this. You ought to be in a rest home. How long have they been coming? He listened hard, cracking the window to hear better. The snow was still falling in the pitch dark. It was nearly six p.m. No wind. The whine and growl of the sleds strengthened, then faded as they wound along the frozen coils of the Alugiak, blocked at times by the forested banks, clear at others when they ran in the open. Still five miles away, he thought. They should be at the sign pretty soon.

POSTED. NO FEDS, NO OILIES.
SURVIVORS WILL BE PROSECUTED.
J. SLADE.

He looked down to where the detonator wire came in through the hole he'd drilled beside the door. Better hook up now. He took the exploder from his parka pocket and hunkered down beside the wire, bending the contacts to the terminals but leaving the handle locked. The exploder was small, hand-sized, and with a squeeze on the handle the rotors inside it would generate enough spark to fire the blasting cap at the business end. The snow had covered the det cord and plastique he'd run days earlier for his surprise.

He brought the M-79 and the Ruger over to the window and loaded them, laying an open box of shells and half a dozen grenade cartridges within easy reach. The switch that would throw on the spotlights was right over his head. Do you have everything you'll need? You'd better, you old fart.

Too late now to go scrambling. He wondered how they would be armed. He hoped Healey would be with them.

"Mister Slade." The voice boomed through a bullhorn out of the dark. "My name is Danforth and I represent the United States Department of the Interior. I have an order signed by Circuit Judge Albin Dean in Juneau requiring that you quit these premises. These lands are now Federal property. You have been properly recompensed for them. You must leave this wilderness forthwith or I will be forced to evict you physically." The bullhorn squealed like an electronic moose as the speaker finished.

Slade lay quiet.

At least six of them up on the bank, he thought. Maybe seven. I didn't make it more than half a dozen sleds, though. Let's hope they haven't left anyone down on the ice where they're parked. Two hundred yards to where they're standing. He glanced down at the sight of the M-79 and adjusted it to 100 yards. Enough to get their heads down.

He could see them better now that he knew where they were. They were huddled together, talking, trying to decide if he was home or not. They'd see the smoke from the chimney, but that didn't mean for sure that he was there. He might be out in the dark, waiting, or he might have left the country six hours ago for all they knew.

"Mister Slade, if you're in there, please come out and show yourself. You have five minutes."

The voice was metallic, emotionless, through the loudhailer, and Slade knew that it would sound much the same even without amplification. A cop's voice. Police. Noncommittal. Ready to blast his guts out if he didn't obey. Who'd have thought these fuckers would team up with Healey and the oil company? The glacier was now a National Monument, by proclamation of the President himself. All the oil under it belonged to Healey and Morgan and Mummad.

Slade, get fucked, they had said. You're a beat-out old widower of a mountain man, sorry about that, and your string is run in this country. All of this now belongs to Uncle Sugar and his good buddy Uncle Sam Healey. The nation needs oil and recreation. Get lost.

He reached up and flicked the light switch. The twin beams

caught the men where they stood near the riverbank, black in their government-issue parkas, rifles on two shoulders at least, their faces bone white in the glare. Slade opened the door wide enough to sneak the muzzle of the M-79 out. With the barrel elevated to a low angle, he sighted quickly, making sure his trigger-hand thumb was laid down clear of the breaking lever, and squeezed the trigger. The butt kicked hard against his crooked arm with the recoil and the grenade exploded on contact—a snow-muffled whump. He rolled back into the protection of the logs as two rifle bullets slammed against the logs. The triple explosion set the glacier above them to creaking. A quick look out the window—they were flat in the snow, aiming—six pieces all told. Let them come a bit closer. He saw one man jump and run in a crouch to his right, circling to cover the back of the lodge.

He broke and reloaded the M-79 and chunked another round out ahead of them. Then he rolled over to the exploder, picked it up in his right hand and squeezed the handle. Whirr. Like a kid's toy that makes fire engine noises.

The whole riverbank rose in a flash of hard white, a muffled spanking roar of snow and frozen earth. Within the flash, he saw the yellower burst of exploding gas tanks as the snowmobiles flared. Again, he hoped no one was down there. Then he skidded across the floor with his weapons toward the back door. Rifle bullets smashed the windows and door as he lashed the snowshoes and slid into the heavy pack. He fired one more grenade round straight through the front window to keep them down, then ducked out into the snow tunnel.

CHAPTER TWENTY-FIVE

ACTUALLY JORDAN Danforth of the DOI had a rather mellifluous voice, and he was exercising it now in a chain of well-turned epithets as he lay belly down in the riverbank snow. "McGregor goddammit hump your fat ass over there to the right and get a line on that window. Blackie you check on the sleds. I think the fuckers blew." He scanned the front of the lodge with his scope and saw no movement but socked a round of solid into the door anyway, keep his nose clean. Who'd of figured the son of a bitch had a grenade launcher? Those sleds better be all right, he thought, all the tear gas is on them and the radio and the snowshoes. He heard Blackie bellying up behind him.

"They're wrecked," he whispered, "all the ones that's left, that is."

"What you mean?"

"There's only two sleds on the bank, and a big hole in the ice where the others were."

Danforth cursed and rolled over to look back into the dark.

"Bastard must have mined the ice while he was waiting for us," he said.

"Well, he's not all that good with the grenade gun," said Blackie.

"Don't believe it," Danforth told him. "He could have taken us out like he did the sleds. He just doesn't want a murder beef against him."

All my eggs in the one basket, he was thinking. Dumb shit.

"Snowshoes on the sleds that are left?"

"It looked like a couple of pair, but I don't know if they're busted or not."

"Keep him pinned," Danforth said, and skidded back down the bank to the river. The snowmobiles lay on their sides, skis scorched and shattered, but when he rolled one upright he found a pair of trail-model snowshoes lashed, intact, along the lee side of the blast. A couple of lacings were broken but the frames looked uncracked. The same was true of the pair he found on the other sled. The tear gas, unfortunately, was at the bottom of the Alugiak, along with the launcher. What an asshole I am! He looked bitterly at the gaping hole in the river ice. Blackwater gurgled; wisps of steam rose to the snowfall.

"Holt and Petersen, get down here," he called and then heard the men slithering toward him, breathing short and fast in the excitement of the firefight.

"Jim," he said to Holt, a lanky man who was his best runner, "you take one pair of these shoes and head back down to the truck park, tell them the radio's gone and what happened. Tell them Slade is pinned down in the cabin and we've got him surrounded, we need reinforcements. Get Healey up here. He knows the layout of that lodge and we don't. We got to smoke that bastard out of there." Holt laced on the bindings and slung his rifle across his back. "Tell them to bring more tear gas," Danforth said finally, clapping Holt on the shoulder. "And make tracks!"

Then he turned to Petersen, the halfbreed Tanana Indian who had been his tracker for all Danforth's eight years in Alaska. Pete was short and wide-hipped, a dogged runner on snowshoes whose eyes missed nothing, even in a fifty-knot blizzard.

"Go around to the back of the lodge and check with Wiley

172

if he's seen or heard anything back there," Danforth told the Indian. "Then head up to this ridge—" he fumbled a map out of his parka pocket and spread it before them, "—up here back of the place. You'll have a good view of the whole layout from up there. He might have split before Wiley got in place. Check for sign. If you find tracks, give us two blasts on your whistle—you got your whistle, Pete? good—and if no tracks, just hang tough. We got reinforcements coming. Okay?"

Petersen nodded, busy with his bindings, and then shuffled off down the bank to circle in behind the lodge. Danforth bellied back up to where Blackie lay watching the dark blot of the lodge.

"Anything?"

"Dead quiet. Was there any coffee on those sleds?"

"In the river," Danforth told him.

A brisk wind worked the top of the ridge where Slade lay under the snow-heavy branches of a big spruce. He could see the lodge beneath him, and the dark shapes of the men surrounding it, as well as the mouth of the snow tunnel a hundred yards below his hide. A pink line scored the broken peaks of the Dead Mounties to the southeast and the black night had gone a kind of Prussian blue. He watched the tracker picking his way up and across the face of the ridge, quartering like a gun dog. Moves like an Indian, he thought. I hope the fucker can't track like one. If it looks like he can, I'd better make dog meat out of him. He slid the Ruger forward and removed the lens caps from either end of the scope, then glassed the man. The face was wide-cheeked and dark, Indian all right, very serious. He wore a muskrat-hide parka with a wolf or wolverine ruff on his hood, homemade, not regulation. A carbine peeked over his shoulder, the front sight hooded also, against the snow. Slade laid the post of the scope sight on the man's chest, then on his throat and finally on his ear. At this range, it would be a cinch.

The Indian spotted the mouth of the tunnel and froze. Then he crouched and unslung the carbine—looked like a .44 Mag Ruger at this distance, four-power scope. A stopper, sure as shit. How insubstantial he looks through the scope, two-dimensional, like something projected on a white wall! Then the Indian saw the trails. In the days while he waited for the Feds to come, Slade had gotten his legs in shape by running out in different directions on his snowshoes from the mouth of the tunnel. A good tracker would be able to tell the old tracks from this morning's, but the breeze on the ridge had helped: it had filled the fresh trail with light drifting snow, enough to delay the man for a while as he brushed out the drift and compared the bite of the snowshoes frames for age.

The Indian pulled the hood back off his head and scratched, his face screwed in puzzlement. Slade smiled. No, he couldn't lunch this woebegone bastard. He eased back under the spruce boughs to where his pack stood, slipped the straps over his shoulders and walked backward along his trail deeper into the woods. It would take time now for the rest of them to come up. He'd make use of it. He turned his face to the west, into the wind, and began to run, short lurching steps with the pack bobbing on his back so that he grunted happily to himself at every stride.

"Christ, it's a freaking maze," said Danforth. "Which one is the fresh one?"

"Can't be sure just yet," said Petersen. "Looks like a giant snowshoe rabbit flipped out up here, don't it? One hare can make the tracks of fifty, give him a little time." He stooped down and flicked blown snow out of the track, then studied the outline of the print beneath it. "This one's older, I think, than that one back there." He gestured over his shoulder to the crosshatch of trails behind them.

At Petersen's whistle signal, Danforth had left two men at the lodge—with orders to brew up some coffee, damn quick, if they could find it—and then joined Petersen on the ridgetop. Now, an hour later, he had finished two cups and was working on a third. That bastard could be halfway to Whitehorse by now, he cursed to himself. Or he could be waiting to zap us?

"Okay," he said finally, "let's range out and look for something conclusive in the spruces."

"Worse in there," said Pete. "This wind's knocked down snow from the branches, trails filled deeper in there than out here."

The sun was already over the peaks, the glacier gleaming pale blue under its snow shroud, by the time the Indian was satisfied that he'd found Slade's newest trail. They pounded out along it, with Petersen breaking trail and the others wallowing and sweating snowshoeless behind him, their weight dropping them through the layers of crust sometimes waistdeep. From the ridge, which paralleled the river, they could see a party of men heading upriver toward them on the snow, riding snowmobiles and two ATVs. The group was still two miles away, Danforth reckoned.

"Pete," he said, "you cut on down there and tell them Slade's heading to the northwest. Have them run a sled with spare snowshoes up here to us, then send a couple more back to the camp to warn them. He may be heading that way, God only knows." The Indian set off down the slope in a series of long, bear-like leaps that sent fountains of powder spewing from his webs, and disappeared into the dark trees below.

The heavy machinery—D-7 and D-9 Cats, a JD-550 tractor, a grader and two earthmoving trucks—huddled together on the plateau like big yellow bugs against the cold, their hoods and roofs crowned high and domelike with snow. Slade rolled two barrels of diesel out from under the brush pile where he had hidden them and set them up in the middle of the truck park, then lugged gas cans out from another cache in a snowbank over the lip of the plateau. He had arrived within sight of the camp just as the last of the Feds was leaving. The man had scanned the hills with binoculars before locking the door to the quonset which served as their dormitory and kitchen. What's he lock it for? Against bears? Probably some federal regulation.

Working quickly against time, Slade pumped a few gallons of diesel into as many of the vehicles as his hose would reach, then topped the oil off with gasoline from the twenty-gallon jerricans. He pulled the coil of det cord from his pack and strung it around and over the huddled machines, knotting it every twenty feet or so. Then he took bricks of C-4 from the pack, broke them in quarters, and molded the soft white plastic over the knots in the det cord. On the two flanking tractors, he dropped lengths of det cord tipped with C-4 down into the fuel tanks and knotted the ends to the main lasso encircling the vehicles.

How much wire have I got? Plenty. He molded more C-4 on the bitter end of the det cord and stuck a blasting cap into it, then fixed the wire into the cap, and unrolled it out over the edge of the plateau down to a sheltering boulder bulldozed off by the road crew. That would be his lie while he waited for them to return. He wanted them to see his handiwork, otherwise he could have used a fuse and been well clear when it all blew.

He lay back in the snow on the sunny side of the boulder and pulled a chunk of jerky from his pack, tore off a mouthful and began to chew.

Danforth halted the snowmobile just short of a narrow arête. The wind had scoured the snow away and ahead of him rose trackless bare rock. Behind him toiled the other men, puffing and pouring sweat as they slogged up the ridge. Danforth dismounted and climbed up to the top. He pulled a pair of 7x40 Nikon binoculars from his hip pack and scanned the slope below him. No sign of Slade's trail. They had lost it as they neared the bald crest, lost it in a bewildering maze of boulders and drifts and recent spruce blowdowns, and he hoped that from up here he might see his man.

Down below snaked the Alugiak, and ahead to his left he could see the quonset and the truck park. A wisp of blue smoke curled up from the chimney pipe but he could spot no movement. They must all have headed upriver to the lodge when Holt brought the word. Was Slade down there? Goddam. If he was, the whole outfit was his for the grabbing.

Then he heard the growl of engines on the river below him, and three snow sleds appeared around a tree-grown bend, racing full tilt back toward the camp. Good. If Slade was headed in there, he'd find a welcome waiting for him. He sat back against the rocks and watched the sleds skid up to the quonset. Three men spread out, two heading up into the truck park and the third poking gingerly around the quonset, looking for sign of the interloper. They all had their rifles at the ready.

Suddenly the two heading to the truck park stopped short

in their tracks. Danforth focused on them, his head aching from the strain. They appeared to be listening, but with the wind on the ridge he could hear nothing. Then the men turned and ran back toward the quonset, waving their arms at their companion. All three of them flopped face down in the snow and covered their heads with their arms.

The vehicles, in that instant, leaped into the sky on a shimmering white fogbank that grew from the snow around them into a giant, flame-filled cloud. Truck hoods, tires, windshield fragments, a 'dozer blade—whirling, turning slowly up through the cloud, shining and bending in the low hard light—and then the blast of the explosion rolled roaring up the slope and knocked the binoculars out of Danforth's hands. By the time he got them to his eyes again, the whole truck park— or, rightly, what had once been the truck park—was a sea of orange-black flame, burning diesel that spewed and writhed up into a dirty tan cloud topped with black, a cloud that danced and wavered like a mirage on the desert. Minor explosions rocked the plateau and more bits and pieces flew free. Then the noise subsided to a cheery, bubbling crackle, as if a stew were boiling down there.

The heat of the blast washed over Slade where he lay hidden under the lee of the boulder. A burning truck tire whirled overhead and splatted, sizzling and smoking, into the snow below him. Dude had told him the C-4 was potent stuff but he hadn't reckoned on that much power. He had warned the returning Feds that the park was mined and had waited until the two nearest him ran a good distance away before working the exploder, but now he worried that they hadn't gone far enough. He clambered back to the lip of the plateau and stared through the acrid heat haze. What a wreck! Treads lay unpeeled in the snow, fuel tanks ripped open as if by a berserker's can opener, engines canted cockeyed in their mounts, tires melted or burning or both. He saw the three Feds reeling and staggering in the background. They'd be all right.

He grabbed up the pack and set off down the slope toward the mountains and the forest. He was running well this morning, his legs pumping of their own volition, unaware of the weight of pack or snowshoes, and he took the cold air deep in his lungs as he set himself against the first long slope into the Dead Mounties.

He thought about the Japanese marines. They were there all right. His rendezvous with Dude would be in the heart of their country.

But now he had other matters to consider. Where was the party that had followed him from the lodge? Probably up on the arête, he thought, waiting to spot me and then either send me on my way with a parting shot—they can't hit at this range—or else continue the chase. Either way, he knew he was safe. As he neared the top of the first slope, he heard a snipping sound overhead and saw a spruce twig tumble in a shower of snow. Then the distant roar of the rifle. He turned and looked up onto the arête. The wink of sun on steel and glass. About seven hundred yards, he calculated.

Slade unslung the Ruger and sat back in the snow, his elbows on his knees as he sighted in on them. He had the scope cranked up to nine power and the field was the size of a dime. Finally he saw one of them, taking a rest with his rifle over a bare boulder. The wind was from Slade's left and he knew that at this range it would push the bullet a good foot to the right when he shot. He held low and to the left, squeezed off, and saw the rock chips fly as the bullet smacked the boulder a few inches below the rifleman.

That's just to let 'em know I'm here, he told himself. I could have picked his nose for him.

He stood and walked casually to the top of the ridge, where he turned and waved back at them, the rifle swinging high overhead in an easy farewell. Behind him a black wall of storm clouds rose in the west: another blizzard on the way.

CHAPTER TWENTY-SIX

"**I** *TOLD YOU* he meant business," Healey said. "How'd you get that nick?"

Danforth dabbed a cotton ball saturated with hydrogen peroxide on the gash under his left eye. When he took it away, more blood welled in the lips of the wound and rolled slowly down his windburned cheek.

"He bounced a bullet off the rock where I was shooting," Danforth said. "A chip caught me."

Healey cackled. Danforth looked at him frostily, started to speak, then shut up. It was almost as if this fat cat oilman liked what Slade had done, blowing up their sleds and giving them the slip and then destroying the truck park.

"Those were your goddam trucks and 'dozers he blew up," Danforth said finally. "And the fucker is still loose out there."

"Good ol' Jack-Off," laughed Healey. "He could have plugged you. If he hit the rock, it was just to show you he could have plugged you right in the snotlocker. If he'd wanted to. How come you didn't keep after him?"

"The men were dragging ass and we only had the one sled,

and anyway I have to get word to Washington. The Secretary wants to keep close tabs on this one. Things are heating up since Slade's kid talked to the papers in Juneau the other day. We don't want this becoming any kind of media event."

Healey got up and went over to the bar at the far end of the quonset. He was a heavy man, tall, white-haired, but with a kind of boyish look still to his blue Irish eyes. Danforth had been told that he came up in Morgan Petro as the old man's pimp and personal pilot. He must be tougher than he looks, Danforth thought.

"Someone told me you and Slade were partners in the old days," Danforth said. Healey poured a double bourbon over ice, then another for Danforth, and brought them to the table. The other men were sacked out in the dormitory, or else on watch over the smoldering wreckage of the truck park.

"Yeah, we had a bush flying business after the war," Healey said, propping his booted feet on the table. "Then Jack went nuts over the Rugged Pioneer Bit. He'd picked up a chick down in Gurry Bay and she worked on him to stay in the woods. I wanted to bring him into Morgan with me but he wasn't having any. He had a nice little guide business going for him up here, but he never really amounted to much."

"The girl, that was his wife, right? The one that got killed in the plane explosion last summer?"

"Yeah, Josey." Healey looked away and sucked on his drink. The ice cubes chinked against his even white teeth. His eyes were clouded. "A real bitch, that one. She turned Jack against me if anyone or anything did. Kept warning him that I was out to take advantage of him."

Danforth laughed. "Well?"

"Okay, sure," Healey said quickly, looking back now. "I knew that there was oil here from the first time I set foot on the place. It mucked up my boots. And I knew that sooner or later—later, I hoped, and it turned out that way—I'd get my hands on that oil. Slade and I found this valley together, you know. He had thirty years in it, doing what he liked. Hunting, fishing, running his traplines, living with his wife and kid like there was no real world out there beyond the mountains. He had his day. But that kind of thing won't wash anymore. Now it's my turn to make use of the country, and for goodies that

180

everyone needs—fuel and fun. What's wrong with it?"

"How'd the plane blow up?"

"Goddammit, Danforth," Healey got up and stomped back to the bar, his back stiff and jolting with every step. "Those are just rumors. There was no bomb in the engine compartment. It was simple mechanical failure due to poor maintenance. And simple bad luck that she was flying into Gurry Bay that day."

"Rather than Slade?"

Healey turned on him, hate in his eyes. He carried a holstered revolver on his hip and for a moment Danforth thought he might go for it. Then he took a breath and calmed himself down.

"Well, it would have been easier all around if Slade had been flying. But it worked out anyway, didn't it? The Secretary saw fit to recommend that the glacier be preserved for posterity as a National Monument, the sole remaining stomping grounds of the Great Blue Glacier Bear, and thanks to our environmental impact statement, there's no problems in a directional drilling operation to utilize the vast oil reserve beneath the glacier. Or whatever the report says. Hell, once we've got the son of a bitch drilled, you won't even know we're here. We'll mask the pumps with fake rocks and bury the pipeline. All that will be visible of our presence is the road, and that'll bring bird-watchers and bear lovers and campers directly to the beautiful scenery. You're happy: I'm happy. Like that." He grinned his wide happy grin and for a moment Danforth thought he looked like somebody else—who was it? Some old movie actor or other.

"Whatever," Danforth said. Outside the blizzard was howling, and he wondered if he shouldn't send some men out to relieve the watch. Or maybe bring it in altogether. Slade wouldn't be moving in this weather.

"What do we do next?" Healey asked.

"Can't fly in this weather, and it looks like it'll blow all of tomorrow, maybe the next day as well. Once it clears, though, I'm going to call in some choppers and we'll see if we can't locate him."

"You'll never find him in the Dead Mounties," Healey said. Again, he seemed almost happy about it. "Too high for helicopters, all kinds of crazy crosscurrents in there. The country is a jumble, with no two valleys running the same direction. Frankly, I don't think Jack will bother us anymore. He wanted to make his gesture of defiance and blow up a bit of our property. I figure he'll be content with that and take off for Canada."

"We've got to go after him," Danforth said. "He destroyed government property and wounded a government agent. He'll have to stand trial for that."

Healey took his drink over to the woodstove and warmed his backside. The wind hooted and whistled outside the quonset. Healey wondered what his old buddy made of the weather.

CHAPTER TWENTY-SEVEN

S*LADE LAY* snug in his down-filled sleeping bag, his head cushioned by the bulky pack, under an uprooted cedar deep in the intervales of the Dead Mounties. He had made fifteen miles since leaving the site of the bombing, most of it through the fury of the blizzard. Along the way he had spotted three grouse huddled in a spruce thicket and clubbed them for his dinner, which he cooked over a fire fueled with small chunks of C-4 and spruce sticks. The grouse would last him until the storm ended. No one would be following him, he figured. He hoped that Dude hadn't got caught in the weather.

Toward evening the following day, the wind backed to the south and the snow let up. He set out, following a compass course to the northeast. The mountains were empty—not even a raven flapping over the blanket of new snow that turned the whole world white. The aurora came out, allowing him to move faster than he would have if it had been total darkness, and he made good time. By sundown the next afternoon he was nearing the rendezvous, and he paused in his progress to climb a small peak and scout the country ahead. Below him lay a heavily wooded valley with a frozen stream bisecting it. A curl of woodsmoke rose from an oxbow of the stream and looking through the scope he could just see the wingtip of Dude's Piper showing at the far edge of the woodline. Good, the kid had made it.

In fact, he was waiting as Slade slogged in, a crooked grin on his face and a cup of hot rum steaming in his hand. He was an ugly young man with a face like a monkey-fist knot and thick, Coke-bottle glasses, small in stature like his father but wiry. He stood hip-shot, his bandy legs bowed in worn Levis, his stained brown Stetson cocked back on his forehead. As always, he was wearing cowboy gear, and a dirty green down-filled vest over his Western-style wool shirt. He fancied himself a cowpoke, always had, and that's why people in Alaska called him Dude. He was, however, the best damned wrangler Jack had ever seen work.

"You're late, Pop," he said, offering the cup to Slade.

"Ran into a bit of weather. I'm glad to see you got through okay."

"We got in just ahead of it," Dude said. He helped Slade slip the big pack off his shoulders.

"We?"

"I brought Suzy with me. She's in the cabin." He gestured to the low log hut back in the trees. The cabin was one of their spike camps, used for moose and bear hunting back in the days when Jack hunted professionally.

"I don't know, kid." She was a good girl, and for some reason totally inexplicable to Jack Slade, she loved his funny, ugly, hardboiled son. "I don't know. It's going to be rough when we go back in on them."

"She can handle it," Dude said. "How'd it go?"

"That C-4 is something else. It packs a wallop. I blew up their 'dozers and trucks with just ten pounds of it."

"Ten pounds? That's overkill. You could have blown up half of Saigon with that amount."

"You hear any aircraft today?"

"Nothing."

"They'll send something up," Slade said. "We'd better get the Piper farther in under the trees and cover her with spruce boughs. Tell Suzy to finish up whatever she's doing over the fire and douse it. The wind's pretty well hidden your ski tracks. I glassed you from up on the ridge and I doubt they can spot it unless they're flying contours, and if they come down that low they can look in the window."

After they moved the plane and covered it, they went into the cabin. Suzy turned from a pot of stew she was tending over the now-squelched fire and smiled.

"I'm glad you made it." She had a husky voice and a slow, easy smile and she spoke to Slade as if he had just come home from work after a long commute. She was tall—half a head taller than Dude—and had long, dark blonde hair and a lithe, willowy way to her movements that reminded Slade, painfully for a moment whenever he saw her after an absence, of his wife. He went over and embraced her, and she rubbed her cheek against his bristly beard.

"Uncle Jack," she said. "The Wild Man of Carcajou Creek."

"Well, Sue." He stood back and stroked his beard. "Why don't you dump that scrawny runt of a cowboy and come be my Wild Woman?" It was a running joke and Dude took it well.

"I couldn't keep up with you," she laughed. "How did you make it so fast with that blizzard yesterday?"

"I walked all night. The Lights were on and it was easy going."

They sat down at the rough table, a smaller version of Slade's original, and ate moose stew with carrots, onions and dumplings, and mopped their bowls with slabs of heavy black bread Dude had brought from Juneau. Then they all had a slug of rum in hot water and listened, while they talked, for the inevitable intrusion of aircraft engines.

"Where would you live if it couldn't be Alaska?"

They were sitting in the dark, with only the glow of the stove flickering on their coffee mugs and on Dude's thick glasses. Suzy lay asleep near the fire, her hair a reddish blonde where the light caught it.

"Damned if I know," Dude said after thinking a while. "I really haven't seen that much of it."

"You know the Outside better than I do," said Slade. "And you've been in Asia, or a part of it anyway. And Hawaii along the way."

"None of those places."

"None of them?"

"Maybe the mountains. It's still pretty good high up. The higher you go, the poorer the people in the monetary sense, except where they ski, and the less dependent they are on the real Outside."

"Like where?"

"Parts of northwestern Montana, across the Bitterroots into Idaho. The Gallatins and even the Shields Valley north of Livingston. Down in New Mexico along the Jemez River, but well away from Taos. The Ouachitas in Oklahoma, and southern Arkansas. Some of the Georgia and Alabama hill country. On up through western Missouri in bits and pieces, western Pennsylvania, up there near Du Bois. The Taconics and the Northeast Kingdom in Vermont. From what I hear."

"I couldn't go back to Vermont," Jack said. "I been there."

"It's different from when you were a kid," Dude said. "There's wild turkeys now, and coyotes, and more bear than they've seen in a long while."

"It's dead country."

"What isn't, when you think of it? This is dead country to Charlie Blue, and to me as well now that we're out of it."

"What about Suzy? Where does she like it?"

"Vermont. She's who took me there. She had a roommate at school who came from just north of Bennington and she went home with her one vacation. Good people, she said. Like Alaskans. No bullshit. Very competent."

Jack got up from the table and went over to the bottle where it stood near the fire. He poured himself another rum and splashed hot water on it, then brought the bottle over to his son.

"You know how this is going to end," he said flatly.

"Pretty well. You're not going on from here."

"But you are."

"I don't know."

"At first I wanted you in on this. The finish. But I wasn't really thinking. Now I want you out of it."

"I can help you and I will take my chance."

"I don't want that kind of chance-taking from you. You've got the girl now."

"She's as tough as I am," said Dude. "She will take her chance along with me."

"Well yes. But not here. Someplace else. Like Vermont."

They sat quietly for a long while. Outside, the snow was dancing under the blaze of the Lights and the walls of the cabin creaked with the still cold.

"You're going to kill Sam Healey?"

"Yes."

"And the Iranian?"

"If he's there I will. I don't really care that much about him."

"I think he did it."

"Sure he did. Or Gates. But that isn't what's important. Motive is nothing next to acquiescence."

"I . . ."

"Forget it," Jack said. "I don't want to explain. I just want to do it."

Dude finished his drink. He went over to the sleeping bag where Suzy lay.

"You don't have to explain, Pop," he said. "You never explained about the bear but I know."

"Nor you about the war. But I know."

After Dude had settled into sleep, Slade took a notebook from his pocket and scrawled a few words on a clean page. Then he took a slip of paper from his breast pocket and enfolded it in the written page. The slip was a certified check in a six-figure amount made out to John Strong Slade, Junior. It was all that Slade had left save his love. The note read: "I'm going down to the Gulf for a while. This is for you and Suzy to spend while I'm gone."

He tucked the papers into a toe of Dude's cowboy boots. He knew his son would not wear the boots again until he got back to town. That would be time enough.

"Nothing," Healey yelled over the flapping of the helicopter rotors. "I told you you couldn't find him." He cackled gleefully and Danforth, riding up front next to the pilot, scowled again without taking his eyes off the blinding, sprawling roll of empty country five hundred feet below them. They had searched the

Dead Mounties for three days now and seen only a handful of yarded-up moose, a band of caribou in a deep valley, and one bear, wandering the snow abstractedly, as if he were sleepwalking.

The pilot, young and nervous, complained constantly that the air was too thin for his ship, and indeed from time to time they had suddenly lost altitude in stomach-jerking plunges that ended only a hundred feet from the rocks. He shouldn't have let Healey come along, Danforth thought. The extra weight was what made the flying tough. But the old man had insisted, and the Secretary came through from Washington with a sharp message ordering Danforth to accede to his wishes. Apparently the old thief had clout to match his cackle.

"I think we'd better head for the barn, sir," the pilot said. He pointed to the fuel gauges. "We're nearing the limit and I'd like a little cushion."

"Where's the other chopper?" Danforth asked.

"West of us about twenty miles," the pilot said. "He's got a shorter run back in."

"Why don't we vector back over his way and then head home?"

"We covered that part yesterday," the pilot said, not looking at Danforth, "but if you say so."

"I say so."

As they angled toward the ridges and snow cones to the west, the radio crackled and screamed.

"What's that?"

"Sounded like Glowworm Two."

". . . worm One, Two here. Contact. Contact. Receiving ground . . ." Crackle screech.

"Glowworm Two, this is Glowworm One. Say again."

". . . ground fire. Sector Uniform Three. I say again, receiving ground fire from . . . Do you read?"

"Glowworm Two, understand you have contact and are receiving ground fire, is that Charlie? Over."

"Roger One. I'm going in to get a firm fix and then heading base. . . ."

"They've got 'em," Danforth shouted, turning to grin at Healey. Then, to the pilot, "Crank it on, kid. Let's join up with him and nail that bastard!"

A moment later: "One, this Two. Mayday mayday mayday. Mayday mayday mayday. I'm stacking in. . . ." Crackle screech.

Tail high, the helicopter raced toward a pall of smoke rising beyond the far white ridges.

Slade and his son were checking their rabbit snares in a brushy draw a mile from the spike camp when they heard the gunfire. Helicopters had passed through the valley four times in the past two days and not paused or circled. Even though they had heard a chopper working the intervales to their west, they had gone out to check the line, knowing that if the pilot turned their way, they could merely flop in the snow under the heavy cover and not be seen. Even their snowshoe tracks were obscured from above by the snow-bowed matting of dwarf willow and dense young popple.

"We'd better have a look," said Slade.

The two men worked their way up the draw and over the ridge into another long, meandering valley, keeping to cover as they ran on their snowshoes. As they neared the top, they could see smoke over the next rise. They heard another chopper coming in from the southeast and lay hidden until it passed, then climbed carefully up to a point from which they could peer down into the next valley.

The first helicopter lay shattered and black in a wide ragged circle of fire-darkened, melted snow, its rotors snapped or bent by the impact of the crash. The second chopper hovered over it and they could see the white blur of faces staring downward. No sign of life near the wreckage or within its smoldering hulk. The hovering chopper soared up and then warped around to head back to the south, apparently having seen enough.

There were two bodies in the wreck, small black and red lumps with fire-twisted arms reaching at awkward angles from the snarl of scorched metal. A stench of burned pork mixed with the reek of hot steel. Bullet holes pocked the half-melted Plexiglas of the helicopter's broken bubble. They circled out from the wreckage and scouted the snow nearby, looking for sign of the gunner—or gunners, more likely—who had brought the chopper down.

"Down here," Dude yelled. Slade joined him. In a tuck of the hillside behind a stand of brush, Dude was standing over a reach of snow tamped down by many booted feet. A fire had burned itself out in the snow, just the stubs of blackened spruce sticks protruding from the hole shoveled in the surface down to bedrock. Around it, the snow was compressed in long shapes where men had slept around the fire. Dude pointed to other depressions where the men had knelt to shoot at the helicopter. They searched the snow for empty cartridge cases, but could find none. "Must have cleaned up their brass before they split," Dude said.

"Not strange in these parts," said Slade. "Everyone up here reloads. You don't leave your empties if you can find them."

Snowshoe tracks led out to the northwest, toward a higher stand of country Slade knew from his sheep-hunting days. It was a tangled, steep piece of mountain where ambushes would be easy and impossible to prevent.

"We're going to have to clear out," he said to his son. "That other chopper will be back with help and they'll sure as hell find our tracks, then follow them back to the cabin. Dammit. I wanted to stay another few days. I hoped that they'd figure I was over the line into Canada by now."

"There's only six of them," Dude said. He had been crouched over the snowshoe tracks, trying to distinguish one from the other. "Pretty big men for Indians or Eskimos. Could there be a party of white men in here this time of year?"

"Not likely."

"Well, you're right about splitting. They'll figure you to have shot down the helicopter. We could get Sue and track these fellows out, get the jump on them and bring them in. Once they check the bullets in the helicopter against their rifles you'd be clear."

"I didn't want to kill anyone," Slade said, "but I don't want to be 'clear' either. I'm at war with these sons of bitches, both the Feds and Healey, and I don't want it to end now. Not until I've made them pay for their sins."

When they reached the cabin they found Susan lugging packs out to the airplane. The fire was damped and the snow had been blown clear of the skis. The engine was warm.

"I heard it," she said. "We're ready to fly once we get the gear stowed."

Slade walked over to the neat row of baggage and pulled

190

his pack clear. He slung the straps over his shoulders, shrugged once, then laid the rifle across his forearm in the Indian carry.

"Get going," he said.

"What about you?"

"This isn't your fight. It's mine, always has been. I'll move out the way those gunners went. You two get back to town, don't get involved. They want blood now and I don't want it to be yours."

"You're an asshole, Dad."

"Maybe so. But say it again and I'll bore you a new one of your own."

The plane climbed free of the valley under heavy skies. As it banked once to the east and then again around to the southwest, Dude and Suzy saw him waving to them, small and squat under the heavy pack, the rifle tiny in his hand.

"He *is* a proper asshole," said Dude. His hands were tight on the stick.

"Easy," she said. "Where does he have to go from here?"

"Where do *we* have to go?"

"Anywhere," said Suzy. "As long as it's us who make the journey."

CHAPTER TWENTY-EIGHT

*N*OW HE was out in it: the vastness empty of life and heat, only the hard low light on snow and wind-bare rock as he moved through it, the only sound the fall of his snowshoes as he plugged forward. Even the wind was silent. There were no trees for it to strum. This is how he had hoped it all would be, just moving through the high, empty country with no memory of where he had come from and no need to arrive anywhere at the end. Not even the dogs to whip in line, no traces to untangle, no fights to break up, no worry about how to feed them when the day's fun was ended.

He ran each day along the ridges until he was leg-weary, then descended into a valley to find shelter among the spruces. He melted snow and ice over a small fire, drank bitter tea, ate a handful of boiled rice and a piece of moose jerky, then zipped himself deep into the mummy bag and slept until his dream awakened him.

In the dream, Josey emerged from a ball of flame, smiling and offering her hand. The fire had burned away the years and she was young as she had been that first fine summer they were together, alone in the country under the icefall. She stood naked with the fire boiling behind her, smiling and silent, only her beckoning arm inviting him forward. But his feet were rooted; he could not move to follow her. He tried to call out for her help but his voice stuck in his throat and all the sound that could emerge was that of the wind moving through branches, carrying with it the hard cold caress of snow. Then, still smiling, she faded back into the fire and was gone.

He had to run for an hour before the pain would subside, and even then it lingered on deep in his belly, a low ache that pulsed with his footfalls: gone, gone, she's gone, gone. . . .

On the day he ran out of food, he stopped on a high ridge and scanned the country below him. A deep cirque fell off a thousand feet to his left—the southwest—and in its basin lay a small lake, frozen at this season, but surrounded by spruce and balsam trees. The basin seemed big enough to hold wintering game. He pulled his 8x30 Zeiss sheep glasses from the pack and studied the snow for tracks. There were game trails stamped in the snow all around the edge of the basin and cutting into it to disappear into heavy cover. He worked his way down the side of cirque, snowshoes slung on his back and cutting his steps in the crusted snow with his knife as he went. He stopped frequently on the way down to glass the basin. Finally he saw movement: a caribou cow and two nearly full-grown calves pawing the snow at the edge of the trees. He unslung the .22–250 and used its butt as a staff as he continued the descent, keeping to the cover of boulders so as not to alarm the game.

When he had come to within three hundred yards of the caribou, he began his final stalk. He slid out of the pack and circled on his hands and knees through the snow until he was above and behind the browsing animals. The snow here had been melted away by the focusing effect of sun on the concave rock wall and he found the rubble loose under his boots. A large square-topped boulder masked him from the caribou and he would have to work around the far end to get a shot. The light was fading now but still he moved with the utmost caution, painstakingly rearranging the loose rocks by hand over the last twenty feet to the edge of the boulder. When he peered around the corner the caribou were still there.

He eased the rifle forward, took a sight on the cow's chest just back of the crook of her foreleg, and squeezed off. She jumped once at the hit, bawled and leaped forward, and collapsed. The calves spun around and stared in all directions. They walked over to her and nudged her with their noses, then stared around some more. They came toward him a few steps as he emerged from the cover of the rock, then turned and fled into the timber. They were big enough to survive on their own but still he felt the old pang at having killed a female of the species. But her meat would be tender and fatter than a bull's and he needed meat.

A flock of Canada jays surrounded him, bouncing on the spruce boughs and hopping down to the far end of the carcass as he butchered the cow. Whisky-jacks. Camp robbers. But he enjoyed their company. They reminded him of fat, sassy, oversized chickadees and he threw them tidbits of meat as he worked. He hung the butchered meat on a high limb to freeze in the shade, reserving the liver and heart for his supper, then set to scraping the hide. He built a big fire, heedless of the smoke that billowed up through the cirque, and stretched the hide near it to dry.

Then he sliced up part of the liver and the heart and one of his few remaining onions and fried them. He lay back against a fire-warmed boulder and filled his belly, watching the sparks spiral up into the rising, whirling air column and disappear into the light of the aurora which arched across the dark circle of rock high overhead.

The next day he lashed together a drying rack and festooned it with strips of thinly sliced caribou meat which he had rubbed with the last of his salt and pepper. He spent the rest of the day feeding and watching the fire, and moving the meat around as it dried into jerky. The whisky-jacks were back and he encouraged them with slivers of meat so that soon they were alighting on his wrist to take the offering from between his fingers. They cocked their heads and winked at him with big black eyes. Two ravens arrived in the late afternoon but he could not coax them out of the trees. He threw meat into the woods for them, which they cautiously accepted, then croaking their thanks they disappeared to the southwest.

On the third day, with the caribou hide dry, he moved his

camp to the mouth of the cirque. The encircling rock walls ended just a few hundred feet apart and a small, steep creek flowed out of the lake and splashed, unfrozen, down into a broad forested intervale. The boulders on the sides of the creek were frozen and gleamed like glass, and each rill and waterfall wore a beard of ice. He used the caribou hide to build a rude sauna, heating the smaller rocks in a hot fire and then throwing them under a platform of green balsam boughs he had placed inside the caribou hide tent, using gloves made of caribou ruff scraped clean and soaked in the creek to handle the hot stones.

He stripped naked and crouched in the tent, splashing creek water from a birchbark ewer over the rocks and soaking in the balsam-sweetened steam. The whisky-jacks bounced at the peak of the tent and chattered down at him through the steam. When he could no longer stand the heat, he ran out and leaped into a pool below the tallest waterfall. Then he stood in the snow, facing the sunset in the deep far valley, bathed in red light, naked except for the bearclaws.

Nothing.

Only silence, and the crackle of his fire behind him.

That night in his dream, he took one step toward Josey before she disappeared into the fireball.

The next day, with the cruising ax, he built a small three-sided shelter of balsam logs, roofing it with interwoven boughs and matting more of them on the fire-bared rock floor for a mattress. Hunting around the edge of the cirque for more boughs, he found the tracks of a wolverine. He followed them up along the wall of the cirque and over into another valley. The animal was not far ahead of him. It was hunting out marmot dens and digging into them to give a rude awakening to the slumbering inmates.

Late in the day he saw a black figure moving on the rocks to his right. He stopped and watched. It was the carcajou. It climbed a small cliff and halted, looking back at him. He could see its eyes gleaming in the late light. They stared at one another for a long time. Then darkness began to intervene and he made his way back to the camp. He fired up the sauna and bathed again in the sweet steam. Still there was nothing in the valley.

"Come with me," she said that night.

"Not yet," he told her. "There is something I have to do."

"Do it," she smiled. "And come with me. I need you."

"I need you," he told her, "and I am coming soon."

He woke up weeping.

That night, after he had finished in the sauna and stood naked in the cold, he saw them approaching. Six figures, fur-clad, moving toward his fire across the snowfield from the forested valley. Only when they were close and he could see the full-stocked, long-barreled rifles was he sure. Then he saw their faces in the firelight. Old, scarred faces like his own, but beardless, with dark hooded eyes and skin the color of ancient ivory. One of them carried no rifle, only a long-bladed shallow-curved sword. The *katana* of a samurai. They stood in a semicircle around him, their eyes on the bearclaw necklace.

Then a seventh figure came up between them from the darkness behind. It was Charlie Blue.

"You need help," said Charlie.

"One last battle," Slade answered.

They look like insects, Gates thought. Giant praying mantids nicking and nodding to a god we cannot see. Forged of steel, tireless in their devotions, every obeisance rewarded with another stingy gush of crude. *Mantis religiosa mazola.*

He turned away from the oil pumps, their grunt and clack in the lamplit dark, and walked back toward the lodge. Search-lights played on the face of the glacier, the beams flickering highlights of blue and green, purple and red, from the ridged crenelations that soared into the darkness. Back in the gloom stood the trucks and cranes and D-9 cats that had built the oil camp. As soon as the earth was dry after last spring's break-up, the new equipment had arrived by freighter at Gurry Bay. The heavy machines grumbled up the road to the old truck park where Slade had destroyed their predecessors, and began cutting toward the glacier. Gates watched with grim amusement as the big blades slashed through the forest, toppling trees that had taken nearly a century to grow to their puny size in this hard climate, watched the river go brown with mud.

Dynamite blasts shook the valley as the Morgan Petro crews planted drainage culverts and chewed away at cliffs to straighten the route of the haul road. Mile on mile of heavy steel pipe stretched back from the glacier toward Gurry Bay, where a new dock facility was being built to accommodate the tankers that would soon carry away the riches that lay under the ice. For a while the work crews had enjoyed good, though illegal, hunting during their off hours. They gunned down moose and bear, ducks and geese and ptarmigan, even killed a few caribou up Carcajou Creek, the last of the woodland caribou left in these parts. Danforth, the Park Service boss, looked the other way. He too enjoyed fresh meat. But now all the game was gone. They had seen not a single glacier bear up on the ice. Gates had to laugh. A National Monument to a vanished species.

Tomorrow was the big day. The official opening of the new pipeline. The oil had come in even earlier than predicted, only a month and a half after the first drill bit spudded in. Healey and Mummad-Afi were delighted, congratulating each other ceaselessly on their perspicacity and good fortune. Only Jep Morgan seemed subdued. An old man, he did not like the changes that had taken place at his favorite retreat. Still, it was big money and that was the best consolation. Gates himself rather enjoyed the despoliation. He had seen so many beautiful places ruined in his lifetime—the England of his boyhood gone now to sniveling high-rise senility, the endless golden-green gamelands of Africa burned out by civil wars and denuded of wildlife by poachers. Now it was Alaska's turn.

At first this destruction of the old and the beautiful had enraged him. He had fought on the side of those who had kept Africa underpopulated, a game park for wealthy Westerners. But even now they appeared to prefer profit to permanence. The Arabs were even worse. They seemed happiest driving through deserts in air-conditioned Rolls-Royces, from one pleasure dome to another. So he had joined them, he and his guns, though the only pleasure he could now find in life was the sour one of seeing it die all around him.

The one thing that worried him about tomorrow, and at the same time kept him hopeful for excitement, was Slade's disappearance. Since his raid on the truck park and his shooting down of the helicopter, he had vanished from the country.

That business with the woman, though. It still made him sick to think of it. Not her death, no, nothing wrong with that. But all that effort gone to waste. He had warned Mummad against it from the start, but Mummad had insisted. Not content with having stripped Slade of the country he held so dear, he had to kill him to boot. Gates had come upriver in a jetboat from Gurry Bay under cover of darkness. He had planted the bomb in the engine of the Super Cub with the utmost of stealth. Not even a snarl from the goddamned dogs. Slade was scheduled to fly into Gurry Bay the next day to pick up a planeload of fishing clients. The king salmon run was on. Who would have thought the woman would pick that day to go shopping?

He had waited below the big rapids they called the skookumchuck with the jetboat hidden back in a tangle of sweepers and heard the plane warm up, heard it taxi out into the stream, then the engine up to full revs as it took off. Almost directly over his head the bomb had gone. A perfect blast. A fireball that filled half the sky, with wings and struts and wheels and the engine itself squirreling off in every direction, and the pilot's body—afire and dismembered—spinning out and down to splash hissing into the current.

But it was the woman. And now Slade would not quit until he had killed Mummad and Healey and Gates. Well, Gates welcomed the challenge. He smiled in anticipation of the final showdown. He knew he had the hot hand.

Search planes had been unable to find Slade, although Gates suspected that they had not looked too assiduously, the Dead Mounties being very tough to fly. Though Healey and Mummad believed that Slade had given up his fight, gone off into Canada or perhaps even out of the hemisphere—to Australia or New Guinea, perhaps—Gates hoped he would return. He hadn't killed anyone since Strang, the wayward cowpoke. Victoria, of course, had charged rape. Mummad gave the order. Gates took Strang back into the woods and strung him up with barbed wire, then carved on him with a pocketknife for two hours until the man had simply died of the pain. It had not been very satisfactory. A good firefight was what Gates needed.

He paused as he neared the lodge. From within came the sound of clinking ice and drunken laughter. Healey and Mummad were in there with the town leaders from Gurry Bay—the prissy mayor, Norman Ormandy, and the entourage of pansies whom he had brought in from the Outside to take over all the new, burgeoning service businesses—the Blue Bear Boutique, the IceCreme Salon de Chic, the brothel and the new cinema and the supermarket and the big motel where the cannery had once stood. Gates did not want to join them. He decided to take a last look at the glacier before turning in. If Slade were back and had something planned, the glacier would provide him with the best ambush site. Its caves and turrets and boulder-strewn moraine were excellent locations for gun sites.

Gates let himself through the padlocked cyclone fence and walked toward the ice. There was a cave he had found in his earlier explorations, though he had not ventured far within. It probably dead-ended up in the ice a short distance from the front, but he checked it every day for footprints, just in case it was the entrance to a deeper tunnel or series of caves.

The searchlight beams dazzled him as he moved near the ice, dancing over the seracs and slashing back at his eyes. He put on his sunglasses to cut the glare and drew his pistol as he approached the cave mouth. He stopped short of it, staring down at the gray mud. Tracks. Mukluk prints in the mud, leading into the ice. He stepped forward, his trigger finger tensed on the guard and his senses alert to the smallest sound or movement.

The light danced across the furrowed ice; from behind him, in the lodge, came the pulsing beat of music and the shrill laughter of Victoria and Svetlana. He stepped into the cave.

A blurred streak of silver light slashed out of the darkness, at eye level. A dark figure moved behind it.

Gates never felt the sword that removed his head.

It thudded to the mud at his feet. His body, spouting blood from the neck stump, weaved and then collapsed sideways against the stained ice wall.

CHAPTER TWENTY-NINE

*S*LADE LAY at the very lip of the glacier, on a flat moss-grown slab of iceborne rock. With the glasses he scanned the camp far below him. Workers and Park Service rangers scurried, back and forth from trailers to trucks to valves and pipelines, while others formed an armed cordon around the huge silver holding tank from which the crude oil would shortly flow. They know about Gates, Slade thought. They know I'm here, but they don't know where or what I plan. Let them worry a while.

Behind him he heard a crunch of ice and, turning, saw Charlie Blue crawling toward him. He unrolled a coil of insulated wire as he came.

"It is all in place," he said. "Just where you wanted it." He handed the wire to Slade.

"Where are the Japanese?"

"Those who planted the explosives are on their way out through the rear tunnel. Two are covering the guards, from the rocks on either side, with the grenade launcher and a rifle.

When you start, they will fire and then retreat out of the way."

"You'd better get going yourself," Slade said.

"No," said the Tlingit. "I'm staying with you."

"It's a one-way ride, Charlie."

"I know it," he answered, grinning through his wrinkles. "I am an old man and my country is finished. And besides, it is only fitting that the last shaman should be part of the end of it all."

Slade nodded and began securing the wires to the terminals of the exploder. Nearly a hundred pounds of C-4 explosive was connected to the end of the wire, the packets distributed across the entire front of the glacier, buried deep in crevasses and caves and linked together by lengths of detonator cord.

"Here they come," said Charlie Blue. "See how the Persian struts. Like a grouse to his drumming log. And Healey. He is fat now, and worried. He gapes around him like a thief worried about pursuit. But the old man, Morgan, he is sad."

"Not for long," Jack said. I wish we had Sam up here with us, though, he was thinking. I wish he were still on our side. But he never was. He sold me out long ago, the first time we saw this country. Well, he deserves it. But I still hate it to end this way.

Think of her, he told himself. She was the only one who saw it the way you did. New and fresh, just waiting to be lived in, not eager to give but grudging, yet what a living it provided. Dude grew up in it, he never felt the strangeness or the accommodation. Or the whole reward. He can make his own life, and Susan's, in this new world we built for them. Each of us has to find his own place and make it all fit together.

"Josey," he said aloud.

"Yes," the Indian said. "Think of her. I always do."

"You still have time to get out."

"I am with you." He rattled the bearclaws around his neck and looked at Slade. "This is how it has to be."

Slade lifted a flap of canvas that lay beside him on the rock. Under it was Gates's head. A few flies had worked their way in despite the cold and the covering. They flushed sluggishly from the corners of the dead man's eyes and the raw butt of his neck. Slade looked down at the holding tank. The entire party was gathered at the valve platform. He saw Norman Ormandy simpering among the onlookers as Healey mouthed a speech. A few words drifted up to him.

". . . new era for Gurry Bay. . . . Wealth undreamed of even in the days of the Argonauts . . . time for a change in Alaska. No longer the land of the bear and the trapper, it must now . . ."

Slade hurled the head out and upward. It arched high over the towering seracs, turning and tumbling as it cleared the gray rock-studded mud of the moraine. A good shot. It bounced on the platform at Mummad's feet. Someone screamed—was it one of the houris, or was it Norman?

Danforth and his men spread out from the crowd gathered at the holding tank, rifles ready and eyes searching upward. A hollow pop echoed out from the rocks and a grenade canister exploded among the Park Service riflemen. Danforth sprawled backward, his face and eyes bristling with bit of wire. Many of his men fell with him and those who remained standing broke and ran for the safety of the lodge. The men and women on the platform stood frozen beneath the lip of the glacier, gazing upward.

Slade raised himself from the rock where he lay and walked forward into view. He held the exploder in his right hand, and to the Indian watching him it seemed he glowed as if he were on fire.

"You wanted it," Slade yelled down to them. He could see them gaping up at him—Mummad pale despite his tan, Healey fat-jowled and red with something that looked like glee, old Jep grim-jawed and tall. He could not tell if they could hear him, but he finished his speech anyway.

"Then take it."

Healey's head was back and he was laughing openly now. He could see that the wall of ice teetering above them, with Jack its final projection, would be their icy tombstone. Slade laughed with him. They both knew they were dead: all in the glacier's path were dead.

Slade squeezed the exploder.

The glacier shuddered like a great, blue, bullet-hit bear. A muffled roar broke from the ice face. The frontal seracs shivered and snapped like icicles, their tips shattering and spilling outward and downward. The entire front began to split and tongues of fire erupted from the spreading crevasses. Then the ice under Slade's feet began to tilt, slowly at first, then faster, then breaking up with a groan and a roar as it slipped down the falling face, down into the valley. He felt Charlie Blue beside him, and turning saw the raven climb up and away into the smoke. . . .

EPILOGUE

For weeks the fire burned through the ice, sending billows of dirty smoke into the atmosphere. Flares of natural gas erupted from time to time, lighting the clouds from within so that they glowed red and orange through the darkness. The river itself ran like a rainbow with unburned oil, and for a hundred miles out to sea beyond Gurry Bay the swells shone with its gleam. The thawing bodies of strange animals rolled with the waves down to the Gulf of Alaska.

King salmon, gathering for their upriver run, could not control their instincts and surged in the Alugiak, dying in oil-choked millions. Gulls and jaegers, fulmars and shearwaters, lurched helpless and gasping in the oil spill's grasp. Shellfish died less spectacularly. Hundreds of commercial fishermen, finding one of their last good grounds destroyed, sold their boats and went on welfare. The price of seafood escalated rapidly.

Seals and porpoises, accustomed to fishing for a simpler living in Gurry Bay, fled the spreading slow arms of the oil spill, heading for deep water, clear water. But to no avail.

Outside, the killer whales waited: the only creatures to profit from Slade's Glacier.